ORLA BRODERICK is a single Mother living with her daughter and dog on the beautiful Isle of Skye. She is Irish, originally from Co. Donegal but was raised in Co. Wicklow. She went to an all girls Irish Catholic Boarding school, but was always in trouble with the nuns, so she learned to write as one way to escape.

Orla was first published in The Irish Times. She won The Hot Press short story competition. She has been published in Chroma and PenPusher. Her talent has been developed thus far by Peter Urpeth of HI-Arts. Orla is the founder member of The Reading Room, Skye. She has read from her work on BBC Radio Scotland, the Highland Literary Salon and at The Skye Literary Salon in The Isle of Skye Baking Company. Orla has participated in and devised creative writing workshops. Her writing is poetic prose and is compared with the writings of Dylan Thomas. Mostly, she likes to walk by the river and dream.

The author wishes to thank and acknowledge Peter Urpeth and HI~Arts for their support and assistance with this book.

HI~ARTS

ORLA BRODERICK

THE JANUARY FLOWER

Council House Publishing

Council House Publishing
49 Matheson Place, Portree
Isle of Skye, Scotland
IV51 9JA

British Library Cataloguing in Publication Data. A catalogue record for
this book is available from the British Library.

PAPERBACK 978 0 9574628 0 9
MOBI 978 0 9574628 2 3
EPUB 978 0 9574628 1 6

This book is a work of fiction. Names and characters are the product of the
author's imagination and any resemblance to actual persons, living or dead,
is entirely coincidental.

The quote from Advent, by Patrick Kavanagh is reprinted from Collected
Poems, edited by Antoinette Quinn (Allen Lane, 2004), by kind permission
of the Trustees of the Estate of the late Katherine B. Kavanagh, through the
Jonathan Williams Literary Agency, Dublin.

Edited by Peter Urpeth, Talent Development Manager (Writing), HI-Arts
Book design by Suzan Beijer, Amersfoort, www.suzanbeijer.nl
Cover image DigitalVision

www.councilhousepublishing.com

Acknowledgements

This book would never have happened without Maggie Manvell from Working for Families. She read that very very first draft of the initial first chapter and contacted Peter Urpeth (Talent Development Manager, Writing) at HI-Arts. It was then that my journey, and this first novel, began. Thank you so much Jane Rogers (The Testament of Jessie Lamb), my tutor at Moniack Mhor, for your candour, honesty and encouragement. Thanks to Anna MacGowan for friendship. Thank you Cynthia Rogerson and Lesley Glaister for that support. Then thank you to the Cromarty Writers Master-class – Anne Morrisson, Morag MacInnes and Liza Mulholland for all the encouragement and continued reading. To all the other readers – Gill Roberts, Shelagh Parlane, Julia Rudrum and Marie Taylor. Thank you to all the baby sitters and child minders and my friends without whom I would have given up long ago. Thank you to all the wonderful writers, poets and agents who believed in me and kept telling me I could do this – Roger Hutchinson, Angus Dunn, Jenny Brown and of course, Pete Urpeth.

The lost Chapter Drumlie Dub
http://councilhousepublishing.bandcamp.com/

This book is written for you,
my daughter,
my little snowdrop

"And Christ comes with a January flower".
Advent, by Patrick Kavanagh

MARY, BEFORE

It is the way of evolution that one generation provides for its offspring the thing it lacked itself. And you are here, my angel, and he is not.

We could not speak civilly to each other. As the waves smashed against the house, we smashed against each other. The sea became fearsome. I cursed him and he cursed me. His dark pall mirrored in the water. I soared through these troubles, breathless and full of love. The weather cleansed me. As cold as it became outside, my heat and my fire glowed red for all to see.

Calm times gave us rest, and in those hours he would talk. He would tell me of the unhappiness of childhood, and I think now, in hindsight, that this is where we bonded; this was our only mutual ground.

I have remembered his sadness. I honour him as I raise his child without him. My strength came from him, from his lost years of joy, and I pray to God each morning before you wake that I may face the day with love in my heart and a smile on my face.

1

ROCK FOLK

Bluebottles buzz. The dog hates the noise, the whining of them in the stillness: they are everywhere. She snaps her jaws, clicking her teeth, adding a beat to the sonic whine. Some newspapers lie behind the door. I roll one up and lash out, bash at the air. This is no anomaly; this infestation. This is normal. The municipal dump and the sewage works were built before the new houses. Soon the winter winds will scatter the stink and the insects, but on this last calm day of autumn they linger.

We go out to the shop to get fly papers and peppermint tea. To find a mother-and-baby group: to get out of this house.

As I step into the street a fat woman with bleached hair calls across the street to me. She speaks with an English accent. Says she hopes I don't mind, but she's borrowing the slide from the garden. She thinks it's wrong for the kids to be playing in our garden while we're out. She thought they might damage the plants. Your slide is now on the small patch of dried earth that is someone else's back garden. She says she will return it later. I know she never will.

People stop me on the path. They say: 'my how she's grown. What a pretty girl.' There's soft concern in their eyes. An elderly lady gives us a pound for sweeties. She says she raised three on her own. She says she knows it is hard now, but it will get easier.

We reach the bank. There is twenty four pence in my account. Not enough to make a withdrawal. I count the change in my purse and add the newly acquired pound to the tally: enough for fly papers. Not enough for dinner.

The local shopkeeper knows his market, he has stood at this counter, stocked these shelves, all his adult life. There is a selection of repellents. I buy the cheapest. He chats in Gaelic to another customer. I understand their conversation. They speak in phlegmatic phrases and shake their heads. Her man is dead and her children are all away. They speak of the ones who have gone, remembering the life in the place when they were young.

I resolve to teach you Gaelic, that you may know poetry and always have the expressions of your heart slavering on your tongue. I will carry you up the hills and tell you the names and stories of each place. Your ear and your tongue will be wealthier for such an education. But first I must move to the country. There isn't a bare hill left here with its own Gaelic name still upon it.

I do not raise my eyes to the conversation. I listen like a mute. I steal a meal.

I push you in your buggy through the town to the old dance hall and the toddler group. There is an entrance fee of another pound and I ask if I can pay double next time. We are admitted to the smooth floor boards with toys stretched on their length. You fight to free yourself from the ties of the pushchair. Old MacDonald and his sheep bleat on repeat on the stereo. You race around the room. You smile and laugh. Here in this place of tea and toys and noise you are a shining social light. You beam and bounce. From child to child, from group to group, to each one a hug or a kiss is taken from you. Your tokens to the world are the simple gestures of love. It is all you know. You are so bright and so alive and so tantalisingly happy, while other children pout and push at each other. I do not know how I produced such a magnificent specimen, and all on my own.

All on my own. The utter loneliness I feel in these groups of mothers and babies sipping tea and spooning yogurts. I have no gossip. I have no news. I have no catalogue shopping to brag about. There is no husband or in-law for me to moan about. I do not know the newest Mother, the tiniest baby. I am silent in this clutch of cacklers. I know they will turn on me, turn on each other in moments of anger or frustration, will lash out with their tongues smashing frail sentiments and unwise fashion decisions … just as a few hours ago I bashed the flies.

I attach myself to a two-year-old boy in a T-shirt and pretend with him that we are racing plastic cars along a plastic road. We make loud bbbrruummm sounds and he smiles.

Two hours pass. You and I are covered in the dust from the floor. We are both tired and content from our collision with society.

* * *

Past the pier. Balamory styled coloured doors. Past the queue of B&Bs. Along the shore old boats die, caged fish grow and nosey seals are shot. By the posh hotel. Through dog shite alley. To the sea, to the sea. To the secret garden of the rock people.

They fell from the mountain many years ago. The entire village of stone landed on the path above the cliffs. You find a stick. Your limited vocabulary tells me you think it is a magic wand. You knock on rock. And call out in greeting. Some words I know as English, but mainly it is yabbering. Nonsense ramblings. I translate automatically, in tune with your imaginings.

A small squat boulder has a recess for a door and a nook of moss for a doorbell. You ring the bell but nothing happens so you take the stick and strike the door. One word, a name, is called.

"Kaku," you say.

"Come Kaku, out!" The eyes in your head light as he opens his door and shows himself. You stoop suddenly and pick a little pebble off the ground. Offer it over. And it is gone, taken.

"Songu," you say. "Come Songu, out!"

And the second one appears from the recess in the rock. You bend just then and snatch at a stalk of green, hold it up to the one called Songu.

I sit on another rock, probably another dwelling. I watch. I see their round ruddy faces. They are low and grey. Their ears and noses are large and their eyes are tiny. Hair like heather grows out of their heads. He has a beard that may be some tangled lichen. Faded ferns form clothing.

Their voices are mumbles and are deep and gravely. Like little stones and pebbles being swept through a burn. Like the crunch of a stout boot into a mountain stream. Your voice is the tinkling of that clear water stream. You make light music of the air and Kaku and Songu ground it in the tones of all time.

Drinks are offered. You cup your hands and hold them out, little podgy doughy digits waiting for wonders. You sip, raising your baby hands to your mouth, and you make motions to me to do the same. And I do, I cup my hands together and hold them out. And then drink.

The mouth that was caked and dry is now moist and clean.

My heart slows. My breath becomes deep. I actually feel my body relax; an almost forgotten sensation. The daily domestic duties become rubbish in my head and are discarded. Sanctuary is offered me as you dance in circles with Songu.

Kaku takes me by my hand and leads me low down; encases me with rock; enshrouds my soul with soil. I ask for help with my life and the drum of his heart holds me, offers to me the wisdom of the Ancients....

"Transcend Your Reality."

I take his words as one would take a gift of gold.

Not a second in time has elapsed. You are still in a twirl with Songu. Infected by your giggles, I laugh, giggling like a little girl. Kaku holds out his hand, his great calloused paw. I hold the cold limb and feel that it is smooth, like polished haematite. I look deep into the very grey eyes, seeking the soul of this Being. The whole body beats slightly – it seems it is the rhythm of his huge heart. I am struck by this moment, aware that I have met, and been instructed by, a Being of Pure Love.

I want to ask so many questions and he sees the wondering in my eyes and shakes his head to silence me. He asks me to return some day, tells me I am new on my journey and will not comprehend his answers. He says he will explain later, when I have learnt more of this island world where the ancestors are still peaceful. He says there are many dangers. He tells me not to be afraid of tigers. He warns me of faeries, says they are mainly full of mischief.

You come skipping over. Kaku is but inches taller than you and must only bend his head to kiss you. Songu goes to the door of her boulder-home.

I see now the lie of the village, the paths between the dwellings. There are others, of that I am certain. I strap you back into your buggy. You warm into sleep, and we bimble back to our box.

* * *

Potatoes fall out of the lining of my coat and dislodge the carrots. The onion is still safe in my bra – nearly there, nearly home, stay put, please, dear veggies. I am mortified. I have to bend down and collect the pinched potatoes. I look about me quickly, and coax a carrot back up my sleeve. All day they have nestled in my clothing, the onion leaving a twang in the air and up my nose.

I saw the opportunity as I waited for the old shopkeeper to finish his conversation. I saw our dinner waiting. Now the spuds are spread out on the street and under the wheels of the buggy and I have to scrabble about and be furtive again. I gather them into my coat pockets.

I hate to wake you. My breasts are heavy with milk, about to start dripping. Come, baby, wake up now and let me comfort your cries and kiss your face. Let me change that nappy and watch you toddle about the floor and squidge your soft bottom. I have time now, little sweetheart, dinner is bubbling away to itself, let me wake you and make raspberries on your tummy. We could bathe together and you can slide up and down my soapy body. If I put some Billie Holliday on the stereo would you rouse yourself and dance and jiggle with me?

I sway my hips and run my hands the length of my body, pretending I am still sexy. I shoogle my shoulders and my feet move to Stormy Weather. The kids on the street can see me, peer in and point at the madwoman trying to dance to weird music. I amuse them. I make them laugh.

Bare baby bum, beautiful. We crawl and squirm on the carpet. We listen to The Beatles and I try to teach you the words. We've four stolen potatoes, four stolen carrots, one stolen onion, some magical sausages, and all of it is swimming in a big steel pot with a plate for a lid – hot, homemade food. The allowance for single mothers who do not work will be in my bank account tomorrow. It is a pittance but tomorrow we will eat fresh fish.

I mash stew. You put both fists into the bowl and squeeze. I do not know who I should ask about this, the correct procedure for feeding babies. My way is fun, but not exactly successful. We need someone to help guide us, to guide me in this motherhood maze.

Time for a bath and then bed, baby, for soapy, sudsy, slippery, wriggly, splashy, fun time, followed by a massage. And the draining of the boobs as you slip from this wakefulness to sleep.

I think I am a boat; an old dying rowing boat. I am moored to a rock. I may only sway this way and that. Only traverse the length of a rope. I cannot venture to free lands, only dream a notion of other times, other places. Loneliness has set rot to my timbers. I wish for sails and an oar to help me along. I am wood, made by a tree. I have danced with the wind. I have played with the rain. I have housed birds and squirrels, sheltered their young. But time passes and change is inevitable.

* * *

I wake to the sound of the dog barking, there is shouting and some banging coming from somewhere. The street lights shine through the sitting room window. Two teenagers are bouncing a ball off the side of my house. It bangs on the window and they laugh, one girl, one boy in hysterics. They see me and my bed-hair and they seem pleased. They concentrate their attentions on the window now and aim the ball for the space where I stand. They succeed. The dog shouts again and then hides under the table. I hide under the table, too, to comfort the dog, to think about what I should do. A passing wind of bravery ruffles my hair and I stand and go to the door. Go out, confront them. Only, I am not confrontational and I mess it up. I speak softly.

"My baby is sleeping. Would you mind playing elsewhere, please?"

They snigger. The boy speaks. He is small for his age and his shoulders are hunched like one who is afraid to stand tall.

"You are a fucking weirdo" he tells me. "You don't belong here. We want you out. We are going to have a party when you go. Fucking Lesbo."

The girl starts a chant.

"Devil child, devil child, mother of the devil child. Devil child, devil child, mother of the devil child".

I close the curtains on the outside world and take the drape off the television, turn it on. I spoon dark brown stew into a bowl and sit and watch Coronation Street.

2

OUT OF THE RAIN

He came with the rain, out of the damp grey. The deluge fell down and he rose up out of it. The bright boxes paled behind the fresh aura. A membrane encased him. The wet seemed not to mind him at all, nor he the downpour. He bounced along with sun shining from his blue blue eyes. Nothing could touch him, could detract from the joy in his heart, the smiles of summer days in his head. He was invincible. I thought he wore a halo. I saw some sort of angel stomp through this barren no-man's land.

He was swathed in a blanket. An ancient tartan rug circled his girth and swung about his shoulders. Healthy socks joined hardy boots. One shin, another, a flash of knee and I was transfixed. I gawped out at the live man with two legs, upright and sober and strong and happy, just striding along. Long forgotten rosaries slipped around my subconscious and my lips moved in silent prayer. I willed him in. I pleaded with the powers above and below to allow me to speak with him. Mirth and magic oozed from his pores. I wanted some of that.

He hesitated in the road. He listened (or so it seemed) to the delicate notes of 'Hail Mary forgive us our sins' trail into the ether, and he turned to the window. He saw me. Our eyes met and I was lost. Lost and gone forever Oh my darling. I abandoned my daughter with a bowl of pureed beetroot in breast milk and ran to the front door.

"Thigh a-staigh bhan uisge!" I demanded. He heeded me not and seemed uncomprehending. I repeated in English "come in out of the rain". He grinned and opened the gate.

Had I been wise, had desperation not torn my heart already, had I retained any sense of man I may have paused for breath and thought of this great Highland lad with all the trimmings of the culture and yet none of the language sauntering around Singlemotherville unaccompanied, and I might have smelled the game. It is too early in the story for if-onlys. Or maybe it is already too late.

"Are ye lost?" I said.

"I am not. It is you that must be lost, sister, in this cultural wasteland," he replied.

"You are soaked to your skin."

"That is but a wee shower and handy for washing the dirt of the road off of my plaid."

So that's what it was. The massive woven woollen thing he had swaddled about his body and kept up with an old belt, decorated with a sporran. His voice was deep and echoey. Resonant with rhythm as taught by dramatists and elocution classes. It was a lowland accent and hid some foreign twang. The sound of him brought moisture to my very dry places.

"Take off yer boots and leave them there. Come away in," I ordered, hiding the tremble with terrible strength. I wanted to undress him. Put the babby to bed and take him and stake my claim on him, this vision of masculinity.

"There's a hole in my boot'll make a soggy patch on your carpet."

Wordless, I went to find my best socks, not the pink fluffy ones from an aunt at Christmas but the handknit pair uncovered in a charity shop. To impress him, to nurture him, to show I cared, to give him a reason to return. I imagined the scene where he would come back through the little houses and call from the road:

"Woman, I have your socks and they need a wash".

Meanwhile, he found the living room, the baby in the highchair, the dog waiting for scraps. He surveyed the scene with a glint and a wink and when I returned, he grinned.

"That's a bonny babe," he declared.

My tongue froze.

"Her father will be cross with you, inviting a strange man into the house when you should be feeding the wane."

"She doesn't know her father and he doesn't know her."

Unwitting fool, I supplied the answer he desired without thought or hesitation.

"He must be dead or very stupid to abandon this beauty," he said.

"He is alive and well and lives an hour away but cannot find his way here. He left when I fell pregnant. It was a difficult time. I am a difficult woman."

I did not mean to say so much. Too many words already spilling from my mouth and not the ones I wished, not blabbing the bare truth for that must be hidden deep within. Now he would think me some monstrous creature unable to mind my man or shut my mouth.

I looked about the house then, our little council house, and I saw the mess. The kitchen door lay open and the scene inside, was clear. A sink stacked with unwashed crockery. A floor covered in clarted clothes. Coffee cups and their fetid contents, foul brown rings on every surface.

Last night I went to bed. The daily debris remained wherever it had fallen and I crawled exhausted into my pit. The sound of your snores did not bring the Hoover out of hiding. I was not compelled to clean and sort and put away as you cruised unconscious through faery lands. As you dreamt, so did I. Curled up beside you I shared your innocent sleep. You had one tiny fist stretched toward me, the fat bracelets around your wrist the last thing I saw before I closed my eyes last night. And now I regret my momentary lapse. I tidy at night, every night. So afraid am I of the health visitor; the neighbours; the judges that stroll into my life every day that rather than rest I polish and make perfect the place.

The drips from yesterday's porridge are congealed onto the dining table. The organic cotton nappies soak in their shit-filled bucket in the kitchen doorway. I had neither the strength nor the inclination to rinse the muck out of them, until this moment. The bra, the bolster holder, outsized catapult, stained by dripping breasts decorates the only armchair. The breast pump, unholy torture device glares with one eye from atop the television. He stared at it and shook his head, just a little and went to join you.

Decisions are hard, my little one. For dreamers such as you and me, the choices of life are immense obstacles to be pondered and dissected until all that remains is what must be done.

He was trying to entertain you when I returned from self-mortification to the moment in time. He had introduced and ingratiated himself by emptying the contents of his sporran onto the table. He had avoided the old food spills. A brief history in male fashion was the topic of conversation.

"Long, long ago all the men in Scotland wore these dresses.

And this thing here is the matching hand bag. Once upon a time it would have held oatmeal but I carry my toothbrush and a pack of cards. Here we are, look at these pretty pictures."

You offered him your attention. You studied him with laughter in your eyes and I knew you'd found a toy. I hoped I'd found a playmate.

I washed two cups, put the lid on the nappy bucket and filled the kettle with water, set it to boil. There was not time to do more. There never is the time to do more. The kettle clicked off and your conditioned response was to howl as though set on fire. He was shocked at your sudden change of whim.

"Boobs," I explained. "She cannot see me sit with a cuppa before she has her boobs. It's what babies do, yell for milk and cuddles as Mammy pours boiling water on her first cup of tea of the day."

He nodded.

I scooped you up then from the chair and cradled you. I debated whether to secrete myself away and leave him alone in this midden, or just behave as normal. I chose the latter. Perhaps he'll think I'm Mother Earth. So I suckled and soothed my little girl whilst a stranger watched. You drained one, moved to the other, noisily greedily gulping. Then, sated, you belched, reclined in my arms and fell asleep. Unable now to fake any thing I carried you to my bed and tucked you in. I simply by-passed your room and the cot I pretend you sleep in.

He watched. He sat in the only armchair with his arms stretched out along the back, chest puffed out; observing.

The bedroom mirror displayed a huge woman with sagging breasts. The hair was wild. It was an image of an overgrown beast, the Highland cow. The hairbrush disappeared several weeks ago, sucked up into the house never to be seen again.

Beads of sweat rolled down between my udders, dripped down the backs of my knees. Anxiety – palpitations made pulp of my body.

A man! Fit and well, in my living room and I look like, like, like … a milk cow with too much hair …

"Sister, this place does not become you," he says. In his hand is a pipe. He is fixing a smoke. "This is my pipe of peace, take a smoke with me and chill out sister."

He is foreign – of that I am sure.

"Is it drugs?" my little girl voice squeaks at him.

"It is grown on the good green earth and can only aid you through your troubled waters. Go on, get that into you. You need it more than anyone I know."

Maybe he is German. Waters sounds like Vaters.

"It's been a while," I sigh, and offer thanks to all the angels and saints. "I try and avoid the drug scene here."

"This is grass, sister. It has no chemicals so it's not a drug so it's no bother".

He stresses 'no bother', almost shouting it out.

I nod. He passes the pipe and his lighter. I try not to grab. I don't want to seem too keen. I am desperate of course, but he doesn't need to know how desperate.

"I grow it myself in polytunnels in Devon. I come up to bring my Ma her supply. She has a croft at the arse end of nowhere. I'm thinking the universe sent me here this day to help you. You seem to be the most stressed person on this island. Do you wanna talk about it?"

He has turned more w's into v's. I won't mind a little idiosyncrasy; the man is interested, in me! The pipe, the lighter, the fragrance, my senses jingle and fade. Years and times fall away from me. I inhale again and again. I suck until it's gone.

"Last week someone dug up my lavender plants while I slept, the week before they took all the pot plants. Her toys have been stolen right out of the garden. They fight and shout and beat each other out there in the middle of the street. Teenagers follow us around. They call me lesbian. They call her devil child".

"Glasgow's even worse," he replies. He makes a hard-man face, straightens his back a little more and lets his knees fall open. It is more natural than an act.

"The woman next door is drunk on cider all day and all night. She's on her own with three kids. She threw their toys out on the road and burnt them, then asked one of the charity women to get more toys."

"Shite is a state of the mind and happens to the weak," he says. I had expected a little hint of compassion, maybe an intake of breath or a tut tut tut.

He fixed another smoke, maybe for himself this time, having lost the first one completely. I watched the green stuff, beautiful buds becoming crumbs on the lid of a small tin. He fingered the fine fragments, picked out the seeds and stowed them safely aside. He began snipping the stalks with a scissors. He concentrated on his task. I watched his splayed knees, naked and knobbly. I wondered what lay under the kilt. Was everything about him so perfect and meticulous?

"Amazing what you can find in a sporran these days," I said, my throat dry and my head light.

He grinned again, a big toothy easy smile.

"Have a gander at these your wee one sure enjoyed 'em." He passed a pack of cards, Tarot cards.

"I can tell your fortune." He raised one eyebrow as he said this and I knew that it was a chat up line.

"You can tell me your name first," I said.

"Wallace".

I laughed out loud, snorted snot down both nostrils – the irony of it.

"Is it the great hero, William Wallace, come for coffee on this miserable, dreich day?"

"Nae lass. I'm Wallace McGurk. Wally to me pals and you've not made nor offered me any coffee at all."

"Well then, Wallace. I'm pleased to meet you. My name is Mary. I named my daughter Angel but she's known as Angie."

"She's a great wee thing, awfully big to be still drinking out of you."

"She is eighteen months old and you're not wrong, she'll be needing to kick that habit pretty soon".

"You speak the Gaelic to her?"

"I do."

"Will you teach me some?"

Maybe I got cheeky with the cannabis. Maybe I was flirting. "A bit of Gaelic would do wonders for your image," I said.

"You're dead right, sister, I'd fair pull the finest women if I was reading tarot cards in my own native tongue."

We laughed together and I forgot the outside world. Forgot about you, forgot the woman I was trying to be. Forgot his native tongue was most certainly not Gaelic.

I remembered the boiled kettle, the promise of a mug of coffee. I tried to stand on newly wobbly legs with swimming head and dizzy eyes.

"You're in a dwam," he said, "a Scottish muddle."

"Yes, I think so, but I need a drink. My mouth has gone dry."

He laughed as I toddled to the kitchen and attempted to find the coffee and sugar and milk. My tongue seemed swollen. I struggled to concentrate, to remember why I was in the kitchen and somehow I found a bottle of cheap nasty whisky in the cupboard, saved for teething emergencies, for rubbing into raw baby gums – an old wives' tale to cut down on the howling and to minimise damage to my poor nipples.

"You'll want to know about the outfit, eh?" he asked.

I tried to act casual, tried to maintain some sort of control over myself, tried to appear normal.

"Well, it is a little unusual. You seem to have stepped out of a different century. But then, the accent you have is also a little bizarre. I can hear Glaswegian, Cockney and some sort of American in your voice. You must be well travelled. What do you take in your coffee?"

"Whisky" he said, and left the subject of his nationality.

I laughed out loud. "Of course you do."

I made whisky coffees. I giggled again. Here I am, in this guddle of a house, stoned, with a strange man and about to have alcohol and all before lunch. I smiled inside, handed over the mug, sipped from my own, warmed and tingled and losing control. I felt fine really.

"Tell me, so. Tell all about the good dress. It'll be a better yarn than my maudlin meanderings."

"Sister, I have a plan, a great plan. This wee shite hole you're in is a gold mine for the likes of me. For I am one of the greatest entrepreneurs you're going to meet. I bin about, travelling like. It was Holland I was born, me Ma is Dutch. Hates the Scots, she says, but it is really me Pa she has trouble with. He's pure Glaswegian. I started wearing the kilt to piss her off, years ago when I was seventeen or so, but the outfit's become part of me, a kind of identity. A trade mark. Folks only got to meet me the once and they mind me again. You'll not forget this face, now will you?"

I'll not forget the face but I can't place the accent. He has femininity folded into his pleats yet the boots and the stomp he has are loaded with testosterone. He is a mixture and a puzzle. I would like to find out more. There's intrigue here.

"The folk here chuck out the best of loot. See all they washing machines and fridges and freezers just laying about outside? I can fix them and sell them. I'm telling you, a gold mine, and then there's the bleeding tourists what roam about all over this place, moneyed folk from all over the shop. All they want is to spend their dosh, flash the cash wherever they can, 'cos they got too much of it. Well, I just purchased for myself a cracking bus, an ancient thing outta the seventies and she's a beauty. I'll pile them in from the airport and ferry them all up here. I know this island, know all the weirdy weavers and the arty farty women wanting rid of all the candles and driftwood mirrors they've been making through the winter. Stick an island label on the tat and watch it sell. I'll bring all these city folk on mad adventures through the bog and the moors. I'll tire them out through the day and get them pissed on me pal's moonshine of a night."

He pauses to inhale. He is passionate about his subject. He can see his plan. He is watching it take shape and form. I have no money, maybe he can get me work. The ethics are nonexistent, but there's a child to feed. I can make driftwood mirrors. He could sell them. I could do some small thing, for love and money. I have bought into his plan before I can think of the harm it may do.

"I got a few fiddlers and a fella plays a decent tune on the chanter. I'll be like the Pied Piper. I got a vision for myself. There's a fella stays around here someplace, plays the bagpipes real well and is always in need of a toke. I'm here to make a deal with him. Want him to find himself a good place on one o' these pretty hills and let rip on the pipes and I'll traipse all the fat Yanks up the hill to take their photos. Charge them for every photo. Charge them for each tour out. Find cheap beds for them, make a profit for myself. I'll bedazzle the bejaysus outta them with the good dress as the Big Yin'd say, an take them on an adventure through the Highlands o' Scotland."

I am in awe. I am hooked. There he is, languishing in my only armchair and spouting his fabulous dreams out of his strong mouth. He is handsome and confident and has a plan. I have a plan. This fine fellow is my ticket out of this slum. He could be the provider I have yearned for. His back is strong and straight. His eyes are clear. He has good teeth. He is kind to children. He has money, the wherewithal to make more, and a mammy on a croft to take care of me. The only question left is whether he can satisfy the sexual energy lying inside of me, the dormant, plugged volcano of passion. Look at him with his chest all puffed out and his chin high in the air. He could easily be the King of my small country. I'd be his Queen and his slave.

He fixes another pipe. The tin of grass is balanced again on the naked knee. I may go and run my tongue along that leg and let my eyes peep under his blanket. I imagine roaming through the old deserted villages, the houses cleared for sheep and left to the winds. I imagine tearing the plaid off him, laying it on the ground, throwing him down and jumping on him. If I had any money at all I'd bet he's magnificent under the kilt. The gentle purposeful way he sifts through the grass and the seeds, makes me sweat. But I will have to bide my time. There are better looking, thinner younger lassies may suit him better. There are cleaner, tidier houses.

I stand up. I need to move the jelly legs. I put Janis Joplin on the stereo and do my sexy little dance. He hands over the pipe. I suck and suck and try to look appealing, alluring.

"Mary, why did ya invite me in?" he asks.

"For sex," I say, and take his hand. The grass has taken hold of me. I think I am in a field somewhere. I am acting out the dream I just had. I lead him to my daughter's bedroom and close the curtains. I unbuckle his belt and the great tartan rug falls straight off him and onto the floor. There are yards of fabric and I lay down on it.

We fuck in the afternoon while my baby sleeps. And afterwards I thank him, kiss him and ask him to leave so I can do the housework.

* * *

Early afternoon sunshine catches leaf tips and glisters. A hanging prism casts coloured blocks around the kitchen. Outside the motherwort held the rain like precious tear drops, like only a mother can.

I am shaking, convulsing, the tender feelings fading. My body is crumbling. I want it again. It wasn't enough. I need more. A warm pulsating that stems from sex, my sex. I touched the lace through my skirt. One finger must find the spot, quick, before the baby wakes. There's a terrible heat inside me, a longing. The milk-cow udders felt almost like breasts again. I brush a nipple and the tickle ripples straight to my clitoris. His butt makes seven out of ten, his chest, eight – his teeth six but his tongue nine. Kissing him rates a nine, but man alive his cock rates ten. A few more goes with him and I could teach him how to use it.

An unreal daze drowned me. The mountain mists and heavy

clouds flowed through me. It was too fumbly and sweet for real passionate fucking. Too trusting and honest to be simply sex. My body is raw and aching. I crouch down in the kitchen, between the bin and the wall, where I cannot be seen from the street. I must find the source of all this, must remember my own body. That sacred point of power has all the energy and balance imprisoned. I must find it. The root of me rocks and swells and I call out to the empty room. I shriek to be released. The relief as I came. I remember, he took his fingers to his nose and sighed. I also smell my sex and rest my head on the bin, happy.

* * *

Pick and pluck, snip and clip. Tweeze and trim. Oh! You must stop crying, please. Tweezers like tofu cannot grasp the hair, coarse thicket, stubborn bush. Wailing screeching teething babe, no pill or potion will soothe the gums. Beautify me magic wand, electric razor, depilate, epilate. Scratch and scrape the blade along this leg and then the other. Give me peace my darling please, my arse is up agin a mirror trimming the tangle of bum fluff.

I'm gonna catch you a Daddy to love. Make space around the eyes, shape one brow to become two. Take the dark line from the lip. I am here. I am here. Somewhere beneath these years of neglect I live and I will shine. He will be back. I know he will. The feel of him said it. I will have him again and make him want me forever. I want to leave my tongue on his fair skin, sleek and soft and smooth and honed. Aye, there's the rub, for I am fat and furry.

Ow! I am stabbed. The kitchen scissors are no tool for this

task. I cannot concentrate with all that crying, your outpourings of grief, your howling, shrieking. It sounds as though you are building a pyre with the fires of fury and rage. It is only a tooth, we all grow teeth. And now you are silent for a moment, just long enough to draw breath, to begin anew, a new octave, a higher pitch, more guttural, now despondent. Come and chew and chomp on my once delicate flesh. Find comfort gnawing nipples. No tingles for me now, pure pain only. Let me take it from you. Let me pacify the points of pre-molars, the gums scarlet and sore and throbbing. I offer Neurofen, Ashton and Parsons Powders, Bonjela but, in the end, it's grinding my flesh that brings ease. And sleep, blessed sleep.

I remove myself from the vice of your jaws and return to the window. The mirror is balanced there along with the various implements I am using in an attempt to appear even slightly more presentable – beauty tools, inadequate for their purpose.

Outside, the moon has risen, the little slice of light above the tree tops. I am transfixed by their bare limbs. I see the edges of their spindles where ice drops shine. Not a leaf left. They are stripped and bare and glorious in their nakedness. The winds have taken even the algae and mosses.

My fixation with the arboreal is my Mother's fault. She used to sing to an old tree. When times were hard, when Daddy drank, when Papa died, she went to the oldest yew in Europe to sing, to cry, to lie silent. This ancient icon lives in the graveyard of our local church in Fortingall. People come from all over the world to see it; to theorise and speculate about it. My Mother met it at twenty one, having been shipped from the wild flat lands of Connemara to Stirling by my Father. He loved her. She loved the poetry of his soul, the Shakespearean plays and sonnets he quoted constantly. He drank port, he drank whisky and one day love went from his heart and romance left his side and he opened his mouth each day with a terrible tirade.

'Thy husband is thy lord, thy keeper', he would rant. When it developed into "My goods, my chattels, you are my house, my horse, my ox, my ass, my anything," she would grab me and leave, with him shouting: 'Frailty, thy name is woman!'

She loved the stone circles. It is said that there are more standing stones and prehistoric burial sites around the shores of Loch Tay than anywhere else in Britain. She used to cycle up hills with me jiggling on a little seat on the back. We would lie prone in burial chambers and pretend we were the dead. We danced around cairns. She sat cross-legged and took great inhalations through her nose, forcing breath out of her mouth while humming. I thought she was marvellous. And of course, she sang to that old tree in the middle of the graveyard, in the middle of the village. The Kirk Elders elected to raise a railing to protect the bloody thing. My Father said it was to keep her out. He sulked when she would not raise her voice to join in the hymns and psalms praising the Lord. Instead, she knobbled her knees in the roots of that old Yew tree.

When I was ten there was a great storm and lightening tore the branches. My Papa stole a bough and brought it back to our farm. He made a treasure box for me and a jewel box for Mother. We never told Daddy. We were afraid he would take a dislike and destroy them. Daddy sought Truth in the Bible, said magic was his foe. My Mother studied the Druids and wept, slow and low like the rise and fall of a piper's coronach. He taunted her emotions, her outpourings, quoting Lear again: 'Women's weapons, water drops'.

He sits now in a Parker-Knoll chair in a nursing home in Stirling. After two strokes he is aphasic, silent and drooling.

She has rented out the house, our home, and taken to the seas. She sings on cruise ships, sips cocktails, screws sailors.

And you and I passed this Christmas together, but alone. No Grandparents to spoil you, to pull crackers with, to sing Jingle Bells. No Daddy to dress as Santa and leave sooty footprints on the mat. No wealth of clothes and books and Lego to be spread about the house. There was no family feasting on a great fowl. There was you and I and our dog, the doll I bought in a charity shop, the pram from a jumble sale and more pink fluffy socks from my Mother's sister in County Galway, a bone and a ball for the dog.

If my Mother knew the trouble we were in, she would be here. If I told her our troubles, she would jump on a plane and be here, sorting and fixing, listening and guiding. But her disappointment would be too much to bear. Her sadness for me might crush me. I am as proud as she, unable to ask for help, enduring instead, the harshness of isolation.

The trees are my fibrous friends, my family. Their grain and their pulp are now part of me and I pass this devotion down a generation. Cyclical shafts of strength for the girls. Out there, the branching lines push into the sky and the moon, catch a beam and the silver slithers down, down. The stumps attract me now. There is a difference. I have been blinded. There is something I have not noticed before; that is not a branch but a trunk. It has been there all the time but I could not see it. There are not just three trees, there are six, three pairs. From each base another rises. There are two trees growing from each set of roots, mirror matched, a single beginning for a couple; the same on that one and the other. And they seem to dance together, reflected in opposition, timber torsos bound at their beginning.

And I am only one woman. I have no mate or pal or lover to shelter me in secret rhythms. I stifle a cry.

I watch you turn and mutter. I see your eyelashes grow. I examine the smooth of your cheek with my lips. I want to share the loving of you.

Even the trees have partners. Another year has faded, a new one grows and stretches out before me and I stand on my own. As the trees bow to each other and the reel or round begins, I must prepare to snare that man, that beautiful man. He has so much tangled love to give and he thought you were wonderful. I saw it in his eyes. I saw his dreams, his desires for a family to protect. Those sweet blue puddles that he uses to see, they showed his hunger. He craves, he covets kin and kith. He said as much, whispered that he would return in the New Year and claim us as his own.

2011 is six days old and the problem is that I miss him. I miss the great cock. I fell for him when I first saw him stomp his way towards me. Oh, for Christ sakes, why would such a free spirit as I yearn for the potential pot of coffee already made in the mornings?

Salty stingy water softens my eyes, my lungs heave in shallow breaths. The thought of him has forced an asthma attack.

My inhaler is hidden under the bed in the treasure box like a dirty secret, kept with my Mother's postcards from Santorini, your first curl, our hospital tags. The history of me is here: the keys to the big farm house in Fearnan and the tampons I dare not display in the bathroom. The beads I loved when I courted all that was Gothic; they dangled and clanked on my tiny titties as I straddled a lover. I doubt they will ever jiggle around these succulent fruits. The blue breather I have to open my airways and soothe the cilia, and a photo of the folks with their only daughter – me.

Push all air out, squirt the powder and inhale sharply. Suck it thoroughly through, coat throat and thorax in dust; special dust; healing, medicinal dust. I don't understand this asthma. My parents didn't have it, nor did they smoke, our house was warm and dry, we ate the best of food, we lived in the pure clean countryside air.

We had so much land, acres and acres of fertile field, sweeping down to Loch Tay and rising again into forest – we were rich, we were wealthy we were privileged. Here, in this social experiment, the island's poor scratch and scrape like our chickens on the bit of Government recommended dirt. Oh little darling, someday Grandma may return from sea and throw out the tenants and walk on land again, and we can all three of us live well and safe and dance around the standing stones. But Grandma avoids me. Grandma avoids the care of my dumb drooling Daddy. Grandma is now enjoying the hedonistic youth she never had. And I cannot disturb her to burden her with my troubles.

Outside, someone sings. The super-still silence is slashed by the less-than-sober shouts of "It's a Tinker's life for me." I run to the living room, quietly so as not to wake you again. The room lights are out but the curtains are open. I see the scene, lit well with all those lamp posts. A twenty year old lad cycles a child's bike with a bottle of vodka in his hand. The back wheel buckles and he throws someone's best Santa surprise into someone else's garden, picks up a handful of gravel and lobs it at a car. He is still singing. There is a large extended family of itinerant Irish amassing houses here. His Father comes and puts his bulk and his voice into the air, joining his son in the glory of life on the open road.

The woman whose car has just been scraped curses at the

young fella and his father. His Mother comes out of another house, swaying and yelling and agreeing that it's great to be a tinker. The big man breaks his bottle on her head and she falls down. Her son, his son watches. The neighbour goes inside. I dial 999.

The young fella's wife steps out, a son on each hip, another in her belly and two in care, he punches her and walks into the house. I close the curtains.

Pluck us from this place. Pick us up and carry us far away.

Why have I been abandoned here? It is my secret and my shame. This bed I have made is too messy and uncomfortable to lie in. Why is there no one to uproot this little branch of the family tree and re-plant it in a sheltered space? We cannot thrive here. Dear God and the Angels please transplant us where we may bloom and grow forever.

I am but an addendum in Wallace's plans. I know it. When he told me he could not have children, when he revealed his fishes could not swim, I saw his heart speak, heard the yearning cry for a symbol of masculinity, the selfish gene must reproduce and he cannot. In that moment, his sweet post-orgasm twinkling, I was thinking deeply and I wanted then to lure him and keep him and I mentioned – I just happened to say – I needed a father for the documents: the birth certificate that has 'Father Unknown' is the thing I would most like to rectify.

That is why he will return, to claim you.

My own Father's voice and Shakespeare's words still sound between my ears and my heart.

"A woman impudent and mannish grown is more loathed than an effeminate man."

If I was svelte and smooth he may fall in love with me. He would be proud to protect me too. No more chocolate cake.

Oh, not a crumb. I'll eat brown rice. No mashed potato. I'll put Eminem on the stereo and thrust these hips 'til pounds drop off. The next time he wanders this way I will be beautiful and he will fall for me and take me away to safety.

Oh! Here's the Polis.

3

HULKS

Dark hulks, low on the beach. We sit and watch. Oystercatchers' orange legs orange beaks break their monochrome bodies. Black and white and white and black. They cry and sing. A heron stretches his old old wings. He is wise to the ways of dogs and takes flight.

A solid wall of water passes close by. It makes the sky dark. Herring gulls seem washed bright white against the raincloud. They gleam and whirl and shine and screech. The mass of water takes its dull shades away. It has gone to drown the sea.

We walk. The dog leaps. You cling to my hand, still unsure of your legs, there are so many obstacles to threaten your feet – nicotine coloured vertebrae from long lost sheep; seaweeds and old bottles; rotting crab shells; discarded fishing nets; fish boxes and condoms. The sand is black – something to do with volcanoes, I believe.

A fallen tree blocks our path. Its gnarled brown trunk splays out into fingers. Great knotted digits as if reaching out from another world. It may be the hand of a sea giant, chopped off in battle or as punishment for thieving. We step over the fingers and I swing you up. A breeze comes and the tree moves. There is life yet within the monstrosity, and we squeal and pretend we are frightened of it. I tell you the dark realms have no power in our lives, and we giggle and run.

The dog finds the tree and sinks her teeth into the soggy flesh. It is a fully grown pine that the sea has carried for a while and then dumped here. Centuries of strength swim here. Whole forests felled and floating, borne here to rest; to become a dog chew. Curled spiraled Sitka spruce worn by waves and carved by current stuck! Now! Behind a boulder. Wedged into another world, the life and adventure and sailing gone for now. Our dog tears the skin from the trunk and lollops off with a bark.

We find a seat, an old bench with a brass plaque to the memory of a departed soul. A wishing well honours another dead walker. You drop pebbles into its recesses and the splish echoes and amuses you.

I think about our journey here today and the stale sandwich in my bag. I think of Wallace. I had not seen him since that wet, mid-morning as my daughter snoozed. Months have passed with me waiting for him, preparing my body and my life for him; hankering after the life he could give us, the security and the sex. And then today he just came again, bringing sunshine and a bus full of the first Spring Tourists. I had plans for this day, but the swagger of the man as he bade us to pack for an outing took my sensibilities strolling elsewhere. The cool confidence of him makes me do his bidding.

He handed me a bag, said a pretty girl needed a pretty dress. When I opened the bag I realised it was not meant for me. You are the pretty girl he brings dresses to. It is a thick tartan kilt for a child and a matching vest. The material is the same as his own attire. My dramatic weight loss was ignored. He beamed for all men all over the world when he saw you kitted out. There was no indication that he noticed I had smartened up. He carried you over to his bus, and I heard him introduce you to his customers.

"This is Angel," he regaled as though he had created you, not simply met you the once and that was only in the passing.

When I stumbled aboard the rickety wreck, they were crowded around you, around the man in the plaid and his wee girl – my wee girl. A young lad was taking photographs. An acne sufferer was in charge of all photography. I understood immediately that Wallace was in control, was charging the Yanks for his image, that your new dress was just a show for the tourists. I thought maybe I'd get a few pounds for myself, as payment for my contribution.

He had a child's car seat secured in the bus. It was new and clean and expensive. He strapped you in. I sat down beside you and with the dog at my feet I looked about. There were shelves full of books and maps and leaflets and brochures. There were shelves of cards for sale, basic things with a bit of heather glued on a coloured square. There were rows of bottles of midge repellent. The candles and driftwood mirrors made beside winter fires. There were sods of peat with thin gold ribbon and a price tag of two pounds fifty. The bus was half full of people, well dressed folk with shiny walking boots. He had a plan.

He started the bus and off we went. I had not left Drumlie Dub this past year and I had forgotten each turn of the head brings another peak of perfection, another stunning vista, another picture postcard. We travelled north and west. Sheep, fat with lambs, blocked the roads. We climbed higher and higher into the mountains. The old bus chugged slowly up the hills, out into the moors and the bogs, miles of browns stretching, unending bleak bare tans.

The bus trundled into a forest. The road was only just wide enough for us to pass. Someone asked if we were in a wildlife park.

He stopped the bus. A distant loch shone out, sky blue among brown reeds. The foreigners filed onto the brown, wind-flattened land. They committed the image to mind or celluloid: clear skies, black hills, white tips, brown bog and the shiny loch.

It was just what they came for, the reason the cities are empty of their company this week. They filed back onto the bus, and the engine thrummed again. Higher we climbed. Wallace told us that this land was formed by icebergs, shaping as they melted, carving out the shapes of the mountains as they tore through the land, emptying the belly of the country and bringing it out to sea. You chatted and cooed, gurgled and smiled at all the adoring foreign pensioners.

Another turn of the road and the edge of the land gave way to the sea. Wallace turned down onto a cart track and sounded the horn. Sheep ran scared. Cattle turned their deep eyes. Three men came out of a house and strolled towards us. Their beer bellies led the way. Wallace switched off the engine. I held you so tight you got a fright and cried. Wallace waved over to the old, overalled men.

"She has the Gaelic" he told them. It may have been a warning.

He threw a thumb at me, dismissed any thought or feeling I may or may not have had. He was still unaware that I now had two eyebrows, blissful in his brilliant scheme, his own command and oblivious to the lacy knickers I had invested in. His brawn and clout reverberated around the yard and the hills and I just wanted a soft word from him, or maybe a fumble behind a shed.

The men only nodded. They slapped him on the back, as if he were a son. The dog greeted them with a waggly bum and a metronome tail. She sniffed each boiler-suited man, the pair of orange ones with large swollen noses and the blue fella with his face a mass of broken blood vessels. She snuffled about their feet and smelled them, seemed to know them. They discarded her attentions. They had big fat hands and they used them to sweep away the dog and summon the group of tourists over to the house.

We went through their yard, passed by the ducks and their mud puddle, on by the side of their shed, with a huge dead deer hanging by his legs and chickens scratching the ground. We walked by the caravan and saw the rotting grey tractor. And then daffodils and more daffodils decorated our path to the croft house. It was a golden barrier, separating the harsh reality of farming from home life. We were led into their home through the hall. There were ten of us and I wondered where we would sit, whether we would have a cup of tea here? It was dark, and I cuddled you into me and stumbled along with the rest of the group. We were silent. The largest man, the one in the blue boiler suit with the ruddy red cheeks, opened a door on a woman sitting at a spinning wheel. She was as thin as they were fat. Washing dried on a pulley above her head. Keening Gaelic song swam soft and low from the radio. Tufts of dirty wool lay scattered about the floor. I felt like an intruder on some very private activity.

"Gee," said one of the American men, "you really gonna turn that into wool all by yourself?"

As a group we gasped and held our collective breath.

She said nothing. Instead, Wallace spoke. He had become master of ceremonies.

"Her brothers keep hundreds of sheep on the hill. They use as much of the sheep as possible. This is wool left from last year's shearing. She must spin it herself as there's no way to pay someone to do it for her. They make only a basic living from the sheep and must use all their resources to feed and clothe themselves."

The women reached for their purses.

"As a special favour to me, she has agreed to sell three jumpers she made during the winter. She'll try to give her brothers something else for Christmas this year".

I watched the old woman as they discussed her worth all about me. Her face moved not a bit. She could have been a wax model in a museum, except her hands gathered and teased the clumps into strands. The jumpers were produced and purchased. They sold for two hundred pounds each. I noted a hint of a glimmer of a smile on her face. Blue suit grinned and exposed his cavern of a mouth.

"It'll be a fine Christmas now. Would you folks be interested at all in these wee things here? We were thinking of sending them to the grandchildren, but maybe ye have grandchildren yourselves? Our lot are sick and tired of all the ole woollen stuff, it's new bought stuff from the shop they're after. The woman has coloured the stuff from the moss and seaweed".

He put a box of home grown, hand spun, hand knitted, natural hand dyed baby hats and boots and gloves and tiny jumpers on his living room table. And the foreigners pounced on them and bought the lot. He took cash only.

The spinning wheel whirred and the woman rocked back and forth in her chair.

"A-mach a seo anois. Tha deoch uisge beatha anns an t-Sabhal. A bheil thusa a iarraidh deoch?' He spoke to me, I think. I was the only one not buying.

"What did he say?" someone asked Wallace.

"He said to come and get a dram now. It'd be awful rude of us to refuse. Mary'll teach ye a bit of the Gaelic later if ye want. Would that be a fine wee job for ya Mary? Ye could afford tae buy a fine hat for the bairn if ya had a bit of money coming in."

I reddened, there in the dark room with sadness for the sister. You felt my unease and you began to whimper.

"She's hungry. I'll have to sit and give her a drink," I said.

''There's a tree stump out in the garden. We'll be back for you."

I wanted this favoured son to offer me a seat in this house. I wanted to sit in comfort and feed you. But, he did not see our needs. He followed the cash.

Out we went into the yellow sea of daffodils, and you and I sat on the tree stump and you had a drink. Then you toddled through the flowers and picked some of their heads off. I told you the flower fairies would be cross, that all winter they would have been busy minding and growing the bulbs so that they could bloom for the lady with the spinning wheel. It was lovely sitting there among the daffodils and I drifted off into day-dreams; Wallace-coloured, Wallace-centred dreams. The sunny trumpets seemed to take my eyes, hold my focus; the Narcissus heads smiling at each other's beauty, and nodding in perfection, and a little hint of the man was whispered to me, maybe by those flower fairies or maybe there was a semblance of sense shifting in my stressed-out head.

The way he spoke, the different voices he used for different people, the strut and swing of his skirted girth, the beam and glint of his grin, the arrogance of him, just showing up this day, after so many months without me and understanding that

I would, should, bow to his bidding, he seems so sure of his own power, so confident of his brilliant scheme.

All too soon the crowd came out of the barn and walked towards the bus. I had to pass the hanging deer and the clucking hens without alerting you to their existence. And then I had to listen to their individual stories, the many ways they interpreted what they had seen. They had been enlivened by their experience this morning, their eyes shone with excitement and whisky. Their hearts beat louder and stronger and they felt good about themselves; having discovered this poor family and contributed in no small way to its income. They had no idea it was a con. They do not see the island I know.

I climbed back into the bus and Wallace grabbed my arm. He maybe saw my wariness, knew now that I could see his game. He pulled me low to his face. It was the first physical contact we had made and I trembled again, a little shiver of fear, a tiny quiver of anticipation, excitement at the firm grasp of the man. He kissed me, long and hard, and full of force. He parted my lips with his tongue and swept into my mouth. He tasted like turf, like peat, like musty old places. I was surprised and yielded to him, felt myself enflame for him.

"Oh woman you're gorgeous, get away and sit down afore the hard-on makes me faint away with the wanting of ya. I'm gonna take ye to me Ma's house an' she'll feed the bairn, there's a sandwich for yourself, the ole wifie made them but this one will not sell, 'tis on the turn."

He handed me some bread wrapped in cling film. Some sort of pink paste lined the sides of the greening bread. I noted now that everyone had been given, or sold, some sort of packed lunch. There was a box of bottles beside him – a golden brown liquid and handwritten labels. Of course, I thought, they've been drinking something potent the old fellas make in the barn, some sort of illegal whisky still, brewed from brown bog water.

"Are you taking this lot to your Mother's house?" I asked.

"Only the very special ones, sister," he replied.

"The rest will have the full cultural extravaganza, me pal is waiting on a hill with his bagpipes to serenade their souls with our musical delights. Then we'll hit a pub for a bite and a bit more music, the same pal will play later and maybe even fiddle the night. In between times, I'll take them the pretty route round an about. I'm gonna swing past a few churches and all, let them peer in the windows and hear the bleak word of the God of the Highlands. I was thinking a fine thought about all they Churches and maybe I'll frequent one or two, you and me and the bairn'll find the one offering the most eternal damnation, the hottest hell and we'll join it. I'll rig the gaff. I'll wire it for sound. I'll get a microphone or a tape recorder or something and get all those weeping fraidy sinners lamenting their impure thoughts and keenin' and wailin', and I'll make a CD, record them and play them to the tourists. Course the Yanks'll not know what's happening but it'll give me and my camera man the giggles, we'll teach them some tunes, 'course you've no taught me any o' the Garlic yet, so I'll use a bit o' Vulcan on them and I'll just copy yon island accent, they'll not know, they'll not notice, they'll pay me for the privilege."

I smiled at him. And I kissed him back. And then I did a dreadful thing. I asked you to kiss him too.

He drove me to this beach, and left me here. He said his mother was probably on the beach. He said to go into the house and find food for the angel or eat the unsaleable sandwich. But I cannot go into someone's empty house, but when you've tired of throwing pebbles into the well you will be starving and exhausted. I wonder where this woman is, wonder what she will be like; wonder if there is any chance of a cuppa. Wonder if he will kiss me again?

I crumble the stale bread in my fingers and scatter the remnants on the ground. A robin hops over. Your attention is now drawn away from the sounds of deep water and you try to meet the robin redbreast. You tell him your name. You tell him the important information of your little life, pointing to me and declaring 'mine, mine Mama'. We huggle, my heart is heaving from the joy of you.

The beach stretches away. The sea has vanished after the full moon. The rocks and pools and acres of sand display their offerings, shellfish mainly. We wander through the sea food, the free food. Slate grey mussels, shiny black whelks, barnacled limpets clinging under the bladder wrack on the sides of the rocks. All the different salads of the sea dry and stink on the dark sand. We discuss their colours in English and in Gaelic: dubh, donn, buidhe, black, brown, yellow.

I find an oyster shell and we see the shining inside it and then we use it as a spade in the sand. We look at the prints our shoes have made. You point to the dog's paw prints. I take your wellies off that you may feel the sand between your toes. You chortle. You stomp and dance and laugh. You bury your toes into the stuff and sing 'gone, piggies gone Mama'. I take off my shoes and bathe in the innocence.

The mounds near the sea rise and stretch. I imagined rocks were there but two human shapes become visible, hulks of woman, not stone. All hunch-backed and low they have been there all the while; as we sat and daydreamed, as we walked and wondered, the gleaners filled their baskets with sea-food. The sea has been but a shimmer on the horizon, it must sweep in now and cover all. The women march ahead of the returning tide. Great willow woven baskets of sea offerings are carried on their strong backs. The first is a tall, broad, tree trunk with a straight regal back. The second is round and soft and fat. Each wears a uniform of oilskins and green wellies. They watch us, and then look at each other. Their mouths move and I think they are talking about us. The dog bounds over to them, her tail wagging and drops a stick at the feet of the one that looks like an Amazonian woman straight from the rainforest. The dog waits in anticipation and the giantess stops, picks up the stick with the huge basket still strapped to her back and throws it many metres and our dog is delighted, chases after it as fast as she can. They wait. I take your hand and I stroll over to them.

"It is a fine day" I say.

She raises her head to the sky. So do I. It is clear and blue up there with thin veils of white film floating. An enormous bird circles the sky above our heads. It plays in the thermals and glides easily above our heads. It cuts out the light.

"De Golden Eagle," she tells me, "De Great One is watching."

It takes a few seconds for me to interpret this information, this new voice. I guess she is German. This must be Wallace's Mother.

"My name is Mary," I tell her, "Wallace brought me here, told me to wait for you. He has taken some tourists hiking up a hill, he has a piper ready to play a tune in an old broch and then they're going to a pub and then a Church, I think. He said he would be back after dinner, when he has them all bedded down for the night in lodgings somewhere."

"Well, you must to the house now, have some tea and de baby

will be hungry, all day on de beach. Vall not feed you I think, he so interested in money now. Come"

I have to carry you so that I may keep up with her.

They stride and I trundle up the hill from the shore. They turn onto an old cart track, an old holed road. You know now that food and naps have been forgotten and you fidget in my arms, your little fist trying to uncover my breast that you may at least touch nourishment. Three large white tents appear in the field on my left. A hand-painted sign states that they are teepees, and they are for rent. We walk past a shed stuffed with empty plastic bottles. A board declares that this is the recycling point. A nanny goat bleats out at us and charges. The dog is terrified. The goat is tethered. There are several more, grazing under trees and beside a little burn. The stream is decorated with primroses; all up and down the mossy banks their delicate pales survive the goats. There are small dwellings dotted in the woodland: eco-friendly cabins and yurts. Trees, a grove of tall, thriving, slender stems, shelters and adorns this haven.

We reach the house. It has been a croft house at some stage but many extensions have created a sprawl. A large, laughing Buddha smiles as we reach the conservatory. Shoes and boots are left here, house shoes for all sizes, all shapes are arranged on some shelves. Plants and flowers and herbs grow and bloom and scent the hall. Light floats in from the many windows. Crystals of clear quartz and amethyst sparkle, a wind chime tinkles somewhere.

Her voice calls out, beckons me in and I go to find her. Her skin shines like lustrous leather. Her eyes dance behind very thick spectacles. I can smell the sea and something very pungent in the room – it is she, of course. In her hand is a smoulder-

49

ing twig, a bunch of dried leaves or herbs and it is smoking, it stinks out the room and she beckons me toward it. She holds the burning branch of leaves over my head and strokes the air around my hair, and down along the length of my back. She asks me to raise my feet that she may clean underneath them with the charred flare – 'to clear my aura.' I have been smudged with sacred sage. The other woman, the silent one, has disappeared. I am left alone with Wallace's Mother. She is like a big, ferocious angel. I understand where Wallace got his features. I think she is beautiful. I think her house is beautiful. I think this is a little piece of the heaven I have wanted for so long. I am happy but uncomfortable. My skills at small talk have vanished in the time I have lived in Drumlie Dub. I do not know what to say or how to be. I do not know how to behave.

"Sit down, my dear. I will make for you a cup of tea. Make for the baby some soft fruit. My name is Gertrude. You call me that."

"Yes, my name is Mary. I am pleased to meet you. Thank you for the tea."

"Dis small one is perfect. So pretty"

Her eyes narrow. The slitty, slanty way she calculates my child's beauty is unsettling. I retch.

"The milk tastes funny" I say, trying to hide the reason for my nausea.

"It ees fresh from de goat" she says.

"…Goat?" I ask, with another reason to be nauseous.

"Yes, is much more better for you. Baby must drink this instead of the cow. The cow milk is not for humans. The molecular structure of the cow-milk is too big, too fatty for little ones. You see how I know this, my second husband built a hostel in Holland, on the banks of the IJsselmeer and he made all beds the usual Scottish size. He was a fool. Dutch people could not stretch out and be comfortable as they slept. All these beds were too short. Dutch people drink much milk from the cows. Make them very tall. Too tall. Like giant. Many peoples have allergy to cow. Goat much better. Easy for human body."

I nod compliance with her authority. Her accent is confusing. The Highland lilt has crept into her hard Germanic vowels. Her jaw must approach consonants at an angle.

"I was scientist you know," she says. "I am still scientist of all food. All de flowers have medicine. Maybe you call me doctor. I fix depression with some herbs and some flowers and food, you know? I help with all the fat of you. I take it away. Make you thin and happy."

"Your home is lovely," I say, changing the subject.

"Is also business," she replies.

She tells me that there is a bunkhouse to sleep thirty six people and she rents out six rooms in her house as bed and breakfast. She tells me she has a large garden with a polytunnel; she grows most of the food needed for herself, her partner and all their guests. She has softened two apples in a saucepan and now she blends a banana and a handful of grapes in a food processor. She adds some goat's yogurt and mixes it up, crumbles in an oat cake and hands it to me in a small bowl. Then she passes me a teaspoon and an old muslin cloth. She talks constantly, her jowls cautiously forming words. Her ego fills the room. She has large ears and even they seem confident. The circles under her eyes bulge with self-appreciation.

I wrap the muslin around your neck. I am wary of this mixture for many reasons. I fear what I may find in your nappy later. I fear it may fly about this bright, shiny kitchen as you spit it out as far as you can. But you love it. You finish the bowl, clear it up as though you have never tasted anything quite so wonderful. The one-sided conversation continues. This is a proud lady. She is proud of her herself and she lauds her own accomplishments; praises her own abilities. She says she will massage me later; she can release my negative energies with her special talents; by laying her hands on me she can connect with my pain and call the hurts of my life into her palms and into her body, she then discharges the damaged life forces through belching. My distresses and my sadness will be broken open, broken down and expunged in her exhalations of halitosis. It is her gift to burp out the stagnant waste in another's body. I baulk at the thought.

She tells me she has spent many years in silent retreat, learning the ways of the mind, the limitations of her humanity so that she can overcome the boundaries and difficulties of this existence. With missing prepositions she describes life as a hermit; only ghosts and spirits as company. I wonder if this is why she cannot shut up now? She is a Healer, she informs me. Grown men weep as she belches out their blockages, she declares. The mixed up accent contributes to the bizarre speech.

I tell her about growing up around all the stone circles because I want her to bond with me, I want her to like me and this may be some sort of common ground and of course she knows the place, has attended the annual high council of witches there. I don't tell her my father protected me, warned me of her kind. Her theory that the Stones are markers for alien space ships is one I have heard before. Her specific descriptions of various aliens, is news to me. Constellations are named and their individual progeny portrayed. That she may be an alien is entirely plausible.

Gertrude hands me some cooled peppermint tea in a plastic

beaker with a spout. I am sure you will hate it. Again I am wrong and you finish it. Gertrude holds out her hands for you and there is no reason to refuse her, she takes you off into her music room, to play you the piano.

I follow. Now I see where we are. This room faces the shore. More huge picture windows dominate the space. The last light of this day brightens even the corners of this room. More plants in pots. It is a simple room. It is sparse but many interesting objects catch my eye, art treasures are displayed with delight. There is a marble statue of a very beautiful woman surrounded by dozens of pewter angels. Hieroglyphics and symbols on every wall like the digits on the face of a clock, candles and cushions for meditation. I have entered another reality, a different dimension. I had no idea such places existed. She points out a statue of the Goddess and it is to honour all women, especially Mothers. I am so overcome with emotion that a tear escapes from each eye and my mouth hangs open like a stupid dog.

She plays Mozart on the piano. The dog lies at her feet. You fall asleep in her arms. She plays on. You snore. She directs me to one of her spare rooms, tells me where to find some children's pyjamas (aware that to sleep comfortably in the itchy, scratchy kilt you have endured all day would be impossible) and ensures I have an adequate supply of diapers. The room is gentle and easy. There is a patchwork quilt on a wooden framed double bed. I lie you down and take off the clothes Wallace gave you and substitute them with his mother's. You wake a little, and to ease your cries I offer you your boobs. I lie down beside you and we fall asleep together.

4

TIN CAN

Hold it, weight it, stow it. Our new home. He moved us to a tin can; a caravan on the beach at the bottom of his mother's croft. Our new home is tethered tightly to the ground, anchored with rocks lest it blow away in a gale. I begged him. I offered him my sex. All the spare energy I had was used to make him believe I loved him; to make him believe he loved me.

There in the polytunnel I lay him down between the rows of carrots and kale, on a bed that was made ready for seedlings. On the mattress of mulch and manure I kissed his hairless chest and worked the magic of my mouth on him. My hands gripped at clumps of dung and clay and I smeared him in dirt, rubbing it deep into the grooves and crevices of his skin, exfoliating his body with the muck of the vegetable patch. I took his splutter of seed and spat it in his mother's seedlings, to the delicate, fluttering young leeks it clung, creamy white on the lush green stalks.

I escaped my concrete captor, rose up out of the little white houses and flew away – to the sea. To the roar and the endless crash and splash, the never-ending noise; the beating and breaking of boulders – rushing, gushing, sweeping, cleaning in our ears, and in our minds all day and all of the night. White noise, they say, relaxes.

A sheep track leads down through the bracken to the shore, the three of us now, stepping over the stones. Only the dog is sure-footed. We have to hop and balance. He offered you his hand and I remember your eyes as you declined his help. The wide pools of innocence dimmed and lowered. I saw. I watched. I watched every move you made, but he just laughed, turned to me with that big easy toothy grin.

"Independent wee bugger, ain't she?" he said and I, so needy, so despondent, turned my own cow-eyes to him and simpered some weak reply, betrayed you with silence.

He had abandoned the hardy, holed boots, preferring now to go barefoot at all times. He was more grounded this way, he said, more able, he said, to feel the ley lines. The great tartan blanket lifted in the sea winds and we saw his legs, the puny bleached-white sticks that carried this big man – his neat, white ankles. The motherhood-button, pressed two years ago, wanted to cover those pins with woolly tights, but that would shame him, spoil the image of the highland beefcake.

His opinions and his dreams dominated our days with him, his fierce ranting against everyone and everything. Only he knew the right way, others were inferior. He complained about the way I did the dishes, once finding potato-detritus between the spokes of a potato masher, insisting I clean it with a tooth brush. He complained about the way I hung the washing on the clothes line, said it was haphazard and untidy. Last night he was quite angry that the pizza I had made was cut unfairly; that the segments were unequal. And yet, I know he will want me to remove his boots, massage his feet and grind at his ten year old veruca with a pumice stone. He may even want me to polish his boots. He had bitterness and resentment sewn into his soul and from his lips came a constant peroration. I did not mind his tantrums and outbursts, they were mild outpourings and non-violent. There are worse things to endure.

He did not come to see us every week and he did not stay in the caravan, and I was grateful for that. It takes a certain amount of time and energy to pander to him, to serve him, to listen to tales of his mother, and how she left him. I was grateful then, for many things. We are safe. The solitude is worth the wait. The incessant smashing of the sea on stones is worth its weight in golden droplets of sanity. The ego of the man that saved us is merely the price I must pay.

The dog waits in the shallows for her stick. An arc of water stretches out from her tail. It beats from side to side, catching the sea on the right and sweeping it away to the left, and then right and then left again. The dog grins, shakes her head, flaps her ears and then sits down in the waves. Her personality has changed since we moved. She has become more puppy-like. Her eyes are radiant with life, instead of being burdened with the protecting of us. She bounds and hops and springs. She chases rabbits through the heather, calling to them to come and play. She pounces on voles to make them squeak. She gathers ever-larger sticks in the hope that I may toss them like cabers into the sea. At night she warns foxes that she will be guarding the caravan; that they are not allowed to creep at her door. Her coat shines. Gertrude says she is the shiniest dog in the world.

Gertrude was not happy to have us live here. I have had to promise to work in the bunkhouse and on the croft for her. Three days a week now I clean toilets and make beds. She works me hard but feeds me well. I am indeed losing the fat of pregnancy.

And you, little water-sprite, have never slept so soundly

through the night; tired from all the good sea air and all the dancing we do in the bluebells under the trees. There is a forest here – a government-owned, sustainable pine development, for export. In the afternoons, we walk the length of the beach and up onto the wooded track. You found the nest of an oyster-catcher; the eggs were warm to your touch. We visit them almost every day and the mother bird has stopped screeching at us, knows now that we mean no harm to her chicks. She screams instead at the hooded crow, chases after him, pecking the air around him. She is neater and more nimble than the burly crow, and she often drives her long, sharp beak into his body. His thick black head cannot dodge her attack; sometimes I see a spot or two of red trickle down his dirty grey feathers.

You examine the rock pools, carry shells to me. You bring an old bucket and fill it with debris, save it for a day or so: your precious possessions. Last week we found a fishing net washed up on the shore. I heaved it up onto my back and brought it into the wood. I hung it out between four trees and then I climbed the trees and tied it there, suspended it like a hammock. I patched the tears and holes and it became a climbing frame. I throw you up into it, and you clamber the squares of hemp, strong hands gripping the rope as you climb to the top and then roll down again. I join you and we bounce in there or we cuddle up together. Once we fell asleep for just a few minutes, your little bum poked through the net and you woke with a start.

We do not yet know all the wading birds. The newts and tiddlers in the burns and pools are to be examined and named. Some sheep trundle down from the hill. One white and four black. They sit by the sea and sleep. Big woolly bundles, soon they will have their lambs.

The first day we were here we rolled down the hill after them, for hours we raced up the embankment and turned head-over-heels down again. There was no one to see me and I enjoyed playing, I felt like a child, I felt free. But two days later I picked a fat tick out of your skull, and I think we shall not do that again. It was swollen with blood from your head. I have learnt to pinch them between my fingers and push them into the skin they occupy, then turn anti-clockwise, then clockwise and then pull sharply. It can be dangerous to leave their heads behind in your body; they will still suck your blood. To remove them completely, this little exercise of pushing and twisting has to be done. It is gruesome work and sometimes they burst.

That very last day in Drumlie Dub, as we piled boxes into the van, you ran away up the road to the house of another child. I let you go. I knew where you were. But when I went to retrieve you I walked into a fug of cannabis smoke. The other mothers were gathered at the kitchen table, stoned. A porn video played to itself on the television, and the children played beside it. You were oblivious to the content and I said nothing to the young women who were also oblivious.

We celebrate your second birthday with a fairy tea party. Among the green and blue things of the forests' floor we nibble tiny, honey sandwiches. Broad chestnut leaves are used as plates. The harebells give us tiny cups from which we drink the tea conjured from wild mint. The dog collected driftwood for a small fire. You have no cards or presents, no gift wrapped plastic toys, nor cakes nor candles. We have all we require, and more besides – a roof over our heads; love between us and peace all around us. No one here knows the milestone we have reached and there is no one else to care about us. We sing happy birthday over and over again and we wish and wish on dandelion clocks, blowing their seeds and our dreams every which way. With every rendition you jump into my arms. Your smile, your all-day grin, your baby teeth gleaming, your flashing dimple and the pinked cheeks are my prizes. I send a prayer to help me carry on; help me create the best I can.

We are safe. Round and round the young hazel trees we go, laughing; skipping; singing; hugging and kissing. I am thirty-two and you are two this sunny spring day. Let us stay here forever, let us lie down in the springy moss and never get up.

I remember when you were a butterfly in my tummy and I was on my own on the beach after your Daddy left us. A sheep coughed and the sea slapped the shore. I was talking to you, telling you of life, of loving, of leaving, and all the heartache you would endure. I promised you that I would provide everything you needed, that you would have a life filled with happiness. A car went by with a whoosh and a boom-boom. The little birds flew off. A dark figure drove the car, broke the birdsong; replaced it with thumping music from a bass-box – the father of my child afraid to slow down. His car, a tank, armoured specially to protect him from me. Whoosh-boom and he was gone, the tyres swiftly whirling and the road splattering up. I wanted you to have all the love in the world. I wanted you to be surrounded by adoring faces, peering into the Moses basket and cooing and smiling. Instead you have only me. You didn't even have a crib. You slept next to me. You still do.

Water washes water cleanses, pours redemption, gives us life. A piece of my mind has been stilled by the tide, the endless, boundless waves crashing constantly on the coast of my life. You have abandoned your clothes. You splash in the little river, looking for fish. Your chubby pink body is covered in bits of twig and leaf. Tiny trout nibble your toes and you squeal in fright and delight. I want to be naked. I too want to be a cherub.

Hazels and willows overhang the burn and the woolly mothers yonder will not baulk or blink if I strip. And so I do. I take off my jumper and jeans, my wellies and my jacket. My body tingles in alarm as I lower my bare arse into the stream. I squeal into the tension. You squeal, and mother and daughter splash and laugh, naked in a small river on their birthday.

* * *

It's morning time and there is the usual incessant squeaking of little birds and the throaty gurgling of the bigger ones. It is breakfast time on the shore and in the woods. From here, from the caravan window, I can see herons posted at equal distances along the beach, poised to pounce, one leg tucked into their bodies; they all stand the same way. They know the movement of stretching the neck and tilting the beak when a meal swims by. Clusters of greedy gulls yak beside them, or caw and squawk and hunt above them. I can watch them without waking you. I do not want to wake you. I want instead to daydream out of the window and watch Mother Duck with her fleet of young. I need the quiet to think, to remember last night, my adventure into the world of mists and veils and lunar antics.

The two-year-old tantrums, which my child development book mentions, started the day after your birthday, and my life became a battleground for your demands. I am a little afraid of your vociferous protestations – especially when all you are ever asked to do is keep your shoes on or maybe put on a jacket, or have a drink. These days, if it doesn't suit you, you fall on the floor almost in a faint and object and roar and howl as though I have beaten you or tortured you, or worse. Maybe I should let you loose in the rain, barefoot, semi-naked and thirsty, if that is what you want. I do not know where you learned to throw things, or how you came to know how to hurl offending cups or shoes the length of the caravan. Most days I forget that you are the child I delighted in and doted on, for you have been transformed into a fiend. You are a monster. But, sleeping here beside me, it is possible to forget the days and weeks of anguish and luxuriate in the peace of a sleeping beauty.

The caravan is perched on a ledge over a sea loch. A little estuary of the great Minch stretches out below us. There is no roar today, just a low lapping. A little wind ripples on its surface, sending shivers to skim and surf and sweep toward the shore. The sky is grey and so the water looks dull. The wind-tremors are like the shadows of invisible wings, just touching the skin as they glide over the water.

I try to edge myself out of the bed so that I can go and pee without disturbing you. Slowly I move one leg, one arm, and I ease away successfully. There is no toilet in here. I have made a compost toilet outside. I built a shed from old pallets and spare boards. It is on stilts and it is quite stable. I climb a ladder and perch over a bottomless bucket, then, toss dried grasses and sawdust and herbs into the pile. It doesn't smell, and I am amazed. It was Gertrude's idea, of course. I have learnt how to save water. You will have many recycling skills.

While I am up and alone, I'll try a bit of this meditation. Back in the main room I light a candle and sit opposite it, cross-legged. I straighten my back and suck in my stomach. I focus on the candle and begin the nasal inhalations. My hands sit on my lap with thumb and forefinger touching: this has something to do with the flowing of energies. I don't understand it. Thoughts may drift in and out but they are not pursued, just allowed to be. Only the candle and breathing are important.

The candle flickers. I try to feel centred. I try to communicate with my heart or any other part of my body, but I find it impossible. The activities of last night are jumping inside my head. I am confused. I try to find some sort of meaning or explanation, but it is all a jumble.

Wallace came to the caravan as I was about to walk out in a tantrum of my own. You had spent several hours banging a pot on the walls, shaking the van. You ran from one end of the main room to the other, howling hysterically but I could not allow you out in the rain. You drew on the walls and emptied the cupboards, and all day I had followed you and tried to pacify or entertain or distract or focus you. You refused all of my advances, beating little fists on my body and destroying my heart with huge sorrowful eyes. By evening I was saturated with the stresses of motherhood. I opened the caravan door, about to run into the fields, my face steaming red and my hands shaking, and there was Wallace, standing on the little slope, either listening or just waiting.

"Hey, sister, are you leaving this beauty alone in the van? Are you heading off somewhere better? Will you not stay and chill out with a wee hug and maybe a smoke? I've no plans the night and no place I gotta be. Seems like I'm here to let you out an away from the bairn. Hey beautiful, want Wally tae sing to ya?" he said.

"Your timing's perfect" I said. He didn't want to spend his free time with me. He wanted you.

He has a grump forming around his mouth. His eyes have darkened. This is the voice he uses when he is masking something. I don't go and kiss him. He has that 'keep-away' vibe. I have learned to say nothing, do nothing until he speaks.

"Me Ma's having one of her ceremonies tonight. There's a

group of her pals coming over, bit of an excuse for a knees up, probably. She was wanting me to help her with the food. I had to do all sorts. Here I am, her only son, that she abandoned for years and I am in her house on my one day off and she is wanting me to grate cheese for her guests. I had to tidy for her. I had to make salad and put tortillas together. I never get peace. It's not as if I am going to go to this get-together. It's not my kind of thing. They have all been having some sort of therapy for years. None of it will ever work. Whatever damaged them is there to stay; they should just accept it, instead of all the crying and wailing and yakking about inner energies they do. I think whatever they're feeling should be ignored, there's no point in dragging up the past, just causes a load of upset. As for acting out your troubles and re-living the pain, well that's just a non-sense. There's way too much crying and wailing and talking about inner energies for me. And all the pretending ye have to do. My Ma loves all that, thinking about trees and fairies and fairies in trees and being a tree. I'm no good at pretending to be a tree. I used to go, but it's for women. You should go, get out of here and speak with folk without the Angel following you about. Don't worry at all, I'll mind her like she's my own."

It was a short rant. He did not shout. He did not stomp around or bang cups or doors. He seemed calmer. Sometimes he just needed to talk. You wrapped your arms around one of his legs and grinned. I felt like doing exactly the same. I walked over to him, to both of you. With a hand on your head I leaned into him and rested my cheek on his shoulder. I sighed and then reached up and kissed him on the cheek. The dog came over and shook her ears and wagged her tail and then disappeared into the grass in pursuit of a rodent.

"You're in need of tea, come and I'll make you a brew. This

wee tiny horror can play out here for a while, the rain is not so bad."

He stepped inside and saw the chaos. He took his backpack off and set it beside the door. He went over to the little galley kitchen and picked up the kettle, shook it to check for water and then lit the gas ring, put the kettle on it and sat down on the little wooden stool. Out of his sporran he took his tin and his pipe. A wry, wicked hint of a smile played on his lips.

I just sat. With my head in my hands, I could not flirt or chat. I tried not to cry. I tried and tried to hold onto the tears but first my shoulders began to shake and then snot slithered down from my nose.

"The two-year-olds are the worst of all," he said. "Until they get to teenagers, then they're the worst of all. I suppose it's not fair that you're stuck together all day with no pal out here to take her off your hands for an hour or so. Most women need a bit of space from their kids every day."

He handed me the pipe. Between short sharp breaths and gulps and sobs I lit it and smoked it. He stared at the kettle and it was almost possible to watch the cogs in his head whirr and manufacture a plan. He did not say what he was thinking. He did not offer compassion, hugs or help. He did not talk about his tourists or his plans to dominate the island's tourist industry. He busied his hands all the time; sticking cigarette papers, crumbling grass and rolling joints. The kettle sang and he poured scalding water on a tea bag and picked a thermos out of a cupboard. Then he said,

"My Ma loves the moon, the full moon and the new moon. She has a dance on the night of the full moon. That's this night, you know. You've not been down to her meditation chamber, now have you? Do you even know where it is? Well, you know the field the horses were in? Past the goat shed and past the old wooden gate she painted blue? Have you ever looked down into that paddock? There's a building in there, it's got grass growing out of it. Go on down there and wait for her. Take the tea and these smokes. She'll be along in a while to light candles and shit. Tell her you're stressed out with Angel, say you are needing to heal. Say you've lost your centre or you've gotta find your centre. Tell her you feel the power of the moon inside you, that its pull has drawn you to this place. Let her know I'm minding the wee one and letting you away, but don't let on it was my idea."

I nodded. Tears were running out of my eyes. I wanted him to hold me tight and I felt too weak to go to him. I felt pathetic. I felt guilty that a small child had reduced me to this puddle of pity. I felt inadequate.

"There's a crowd of women that come here for the full moon thing. They'll look after you. They've all had children and they'll know what it's like. They know it's a hard job. And, they'll not want you making the same mistakes they did. Oh no. There's some of them has left their kiddies, not seen their bairns since they was wee, years and years ago. They come here and they howl at the moon, sister, they dance and sing and howl at the moon. That's how bad they feel about leaving their kids. Now, go on with you, go and wait for her and maybe you can have a good laugh at them. Here's your tea and here's a few smokes, you'll need them."

I complied. I didn't disturb you as you dug in the mud. I didn't stop for a hug or a kiss. I just did as I was told and followed the track past the house, down by the goat shed and along under the trees. I opened the old wooden gate, newly painted blue, and strolled through the long grasses in the paddock. There, a big round shed grew out of the earth. Clover and lavender and sage sprouted out of it. I sat on an old tree stump and drank my tea, smoked. I waited. The light left the sky and a chill descended.

They came; about a dozen women. They all wore long flowing skirts. Gertrude saw me and came over. The others stopped and looked up at the sky. I could hear patches of their talk.

"She'll show herself soon."

"Come Mother Moon."

"You have found this place now and so you must come and join in with us. But, you must wear a skirt. I have one, I think. First, I must cleanse you," Gertrude had said.

Gertrude came out of the meditation chamber with a smoking stinking branch; smouldering sacred sage. She waved the vapours around and about me, from the top of my head to the soles of my feet. I can still smell it now, the pungent perfume lingers in my hair and I recall the drifting dizziness I felt and the words she muttered as she cleansed my aura. The drugs and the powerful anointing had overwhelmed me. I can remember that much.

Her voice changed. The thick Dutch accent was replaced by a throaty lilt. She made her voice box reverberate. The sounds came from deep within her. Noises I had heard before but could not quite place. Her usual erect, lofty chin was gone also. She hung her head in almost-submission. She seemed absolutely ancient. It was as though she had taken on a different persona, as though she was acting the part of someone.

I say one of the prayers my mother taught me and go and brew some coffee before you begin your daily destruction. The owls whoop one last time before bed, the oyster-catcher peeps in reply and the tide begins to recede. The stresses of Drumlie

Dub slip like veils from my mind, clearing the clouds of depression.

Last night I think I relaxed, or something happened and I can't quite remember it or understand it. I had always been so protected from the alternative societies, the alien-theorists and the Wicca-folk who frequented Fortingall that now I wonder why. It all seems so gentle and loving.

And you wake with a bound and a grin and two brown eyes that wonder what mischief and mayhem may be created and enjoyed this bright new day.

You are full of kisses today. Or perhaps you are trying to get my attention in any way you can. I am adrift. There is some essential part of me that has swum off into another other dimension. The practical, grounded, earth mother cannot function as usual. I am not that totem of responsibility and activity this morning. I have not yet made porridge. There is no water boiling for bum-washing. But my coffee is ready. It is all I can do to pour myself a drink, hand you a banana and sit and sip and stare out into the sea. I am not in my body. I am standing on one leg in the sea waiting for a fish. I am a furry baby duckling following a mother with a wack-wack-wack. I am one wave in a vast ocean. It pleases you to have free reign of the caravan, I am unable to keep you in check, incapable of reprimanding and you are thrilled. You amuse yourself as I indulge in imaginings.

I am absorbed by questions. The door opens with a bang.

"Well, sister, you managed to rise out of that bed, eh? I could not stay with ye last night. When you came back with the eyes all kind of vacant and dreamy I thought, ach, I'll sling her in to her bed and head off. You looked like you might have slept for a week or so. That's why I'm here so early now. I was thinking you might need a wee hand with the Angel this morn'.

"Your wee one was as good for me last night. We took a stroll out for ourselves so we did and we threw some sticks into the water for the dog. She helped me clean the place. That's what children need; to be kept busy. She knows who's the boss now. And then we had some oatcakes, eh Pet? Did Wally get ya oatcakes? D'ya want more? C'mon little honey, Wally's here, Wally'll get ya some breakfast an a drink. Did Mammy get ya nothing? Bad Mammy."

You are by his side and you wait. You chatter back to him. You tell him colours, pointing out of the window and you show him the banana skin. You repeat "Bad Mammy" again, and it makes you laugh. It becomes the catch-phrase for the day. I watch him remove your nappy. I am helpless. He finds your clothes. He washes you, dresses you. He does my jobs. The kitchen area is spotless in seconds; all the surfaces wiped shiny clean. He makes me tea. The mug is clean; the coffee drips, once a trade mark, are gone. You go out to play. I drink tea. My head is still numb. He makes me toast with jam. I eat that. He makes a joint and I smoke it. He smiles, happy that he can slot himself into my role and do a better job of it. I have not moved from the chair. I am still staring out into the loch. The tide is out and the stretch of mud is busy with curlews. All the skirling and whirling of wings has me spellbound.

"Did you tell my Ma I sent you down to her?" he asks.

"No, I don't think so." I reply.

"Was it good? Did you have a good laugh at them? Bet you'd never seen anything the likes of that before? What were they doing? Were they speaking with you? Were they asking about me? Was my Ma telling all about me? I suppose she was. They women are always saying how awful their kids was, how they were never made to be Mothers. That's why my Ma does that get together. Were they talking to the moon? Were they asking 'Mother Moon' for help? Did you hear them call the moon 'Mother'? Its wild, isn't it? They're all mad. They want to forgive their past. She wanted me to forgive my past. That means forgiving her. I don't want to forgive her. I think we did well out of her leaving us. I was lucky, dead lucky, sister, that she went away and left us. My Granny was great; she brought us up. She's dead now and oh I miss her. She was real honest and down to earth. There was no nonsense to her. Not like my Ma. Granny said she was always a bit peculiar. Granny used to say we were better off without her."

His voice is stronger today. His accent is more Scottish than I have ever heard. He has enjoyed this. He has enjoyed caring for you. It has given him purpose.

"I was meditating," I tell him.

"Last night. It was a meditation, and a journey. We had to pretend to go somewhere inside our heads. I'm not sure what it was all about. But they weren't talking about their kids. Nobody mentioned children. No one mentioned you."

His face darkens to a sulk. He turns away.

A drum was beating. It was the rhythm of a heart – the lub-dub, steady and strong and constant. A very basic melody escaped like breath into the oxygen of the chamber – two vowels, two sounds, high and low. To complement the fall of palm on buffalo hide: A O Ao Ao Ao – long and short, soft yet sharp. The women sat motionless. Lives and loves decorated their faces, their rumbling tones lilted around the walls, inflections of emotions from ancient spirits, and my thorax opened and a passage from my heart made music in my throat. I sang too. A O A O – high and low, high and low. And I sat, cross-legged and still on the floor, and I watched the notes bounce and gain shape and momentum in that space. There seemed then to be other entities swirling into the tune and that is where my confusion this morning lies.

I do not know what happened. I sense something extraordinary but there is no way of knowing. It may have been the grass? It may be the stress of your terrible two-year-old tantrums? The drum has become my pulse. The simple song is now the tempo of my mind. What were the shapes in the mist the music made?

"Meditation can be dangerous. Be careful of it," he said, continuing: "I didn't think a good Presbyterian lass like you would have much time for singing to the sky? I thought you might have a laugh. But you've enjoyed it, eh? You've not to mind my Ma and all that crowd. Have they turned your head to all that crazy carry-on? Well, you'll see, they're nothing but a shower of maddies, loonies the lot of them. Aye, you just go and hang out with them for a wee while, you'll know. You will, sister. You'll see how dangerous all that meditating is."

He is a noise in my head. His whining annoys me. I know he has taken this turn and is sulking because we were not speaking of him last night. I try to look pleadingly at him, distract him.

"So, she was good for you?" I ask.

"Aye, sure and isn't she just the greatest wee bairn ever born? You wouldn't want her getting mixed up with that Moonie-lot, don't go getting her started on meditation and all that. She'll need a good solid grounding in the Free Church, not floating off into space. My Dad was a Wee Free. Sometimes, when I'd come to Scotland, in the summer holidays or something, he'd take me to church. I don't remember much of it now, but as a kid I loved the good fright you got on a Sunday, set you up for the week it did, you could lay awake at night thinking about Hell. It was great. She needs more boundaries too. She doesn't know any rules at all. She needs to be told that no means no. I will tell her. She will learn from me. That way she will learn respect for her elders. I will teach her what my Granny taught me. It'll be hard, but she will be the better for it. And so will you – if you keep your head out of the clouds long enough."

Dust motes hung in the air. The trail of grey smoke from the candles flickered around them. Gertrude spoke in her deep throaty voice.

"The drum will lead you to your Guide. Listen to your drum. Focus now on your breath. And release yourself," she said.

I closed my eyes and began to dream. I sank like a stone into the floor, down through the boards and the soil and past the layers of rock and into the very core of the world. Through a dark tunnel I drifted and then I met some owls. I spoke with the owls and they spoke with me, and all the time the drum beat was soft and steady. Gert's gurgling tones held me, and I felt safe. Then the beat increased and the owls flew away and I came back through the tunnels and the rocks and the layers of the earth and back into the meditation chamber and the little dust motes and the candle smoke had combined together and sparkly specks caught in the light over grey trails whispered with substance and spirit-shapes and flew above our heads and still the women chanted two vowels. A O A O A O. And then the palm on the hide eased to a halt and the group exhaled together and then there was silence.

But that was last night. There is no silence today.

He uses my name to wound me. Sneering and jeering at me, drawing out the vowel in a low, sardonic way, turning his lips up, punctuating middles and ends of sentences with the insult of my own name.

"You are being very weird today, Mary, weird. What is wrong with you? Poor little Mary: the little victim. Life has been so cruel to Mary. Well, you got yourself into this. You did it. If I was blessed with a child I would make bloody sure I had the means to take care of it. I would discipline it Mary. I would teach it respect. But I would never have gotten myself into this situation. I would never be so foolish Mary. Are you unhappy, poor, dear Mary? So, you must join all the other women who will never be happy. Are you sulking about something? Have I done something terrible to you Mary? You cannot see the love I have for you, how I come here as often as I can to help you. Look at you, with your dirty clothes and your dirty kitchen, you need me, you need my help. You need me to come and teach you the things you do not know how to do. You cannot even hang clothes straight on the line. Shall I tell you a few things Mary? Shall I?"

He is screaming now. His face is in my face. I am crying. Thank God you are outside. Thank God you cannot hear this.

"I hate the way you kiss!" He spits out the insult.

"Your mouth is all wet. It is like a fish, cold and slimy. You are a cold slimy fish Mary. You have no idea how to use your tongue. It is as if you are not actually thinking of me when you kiss me. Do you actually like me Mary? Do you? Do you really want to continue in this relationship? Are you with me because you love and accept me as I am, or are you simply after the security of a family?"

He is raging. Storms from the sea do less damage. The anger he has stored, spills out of him and onto me. It is a rant, a tantrum. He unleashes a small hold on the hurt he has held. He attacks me, because I am here, standing in front of him. I am not the one who has hurt him. I am just an easier target: wave upon wave of awful pain crashes down upon my head, his pain. I see it. I see the damage the parents did. He shows it to me, the nub of it. He was abandoned. Now, he will try to push me away, before I leave him. It is all he knows. It is all he has learned. Love hurts. Yes, he is hurting me.

He only stops when I collapse on the floor. Sobbing, shaking. Now, he has the power he wanted. Insecure little bully has transferred his sorrow. He transformed his troubles into a punishment. Now, he is dominant. He is in control. And he walks away with his swagger intact.

You are howling because no one is attending to you.

"I have to remember what the owls said," I tell the empty van.

I go out. My head is somehow clearer now and you are pleased to see me and delighted to take my hand and run along the sheep track into the wood. I leave Wallace striding away from the caravan, and you and I and our dog jog into the trees and find a mole hill and jump on it and then dig in under it to find the tunnel and you know now to how to poke your hand right into the freshly dug soil and along the secret subterranean passage. I pretend to catch a mole and bring it up to your face so that you squeal and laugh and the dog digs and digs and sniffs and wags her tail.

5

HARM NO LIVING THING

Little tiles, uniform ceramic pieces, their sharp, straight edges parallel and perpendicular, horizontal and vertical in perfect symmetry, high and low with no diversion. Inch by inch, row by row I've got to clean the slime from their sides.

Gertrude marched down to the caravan this morning. I was lighting the fire. You were playing in a bowl of porridge and raisins. She was shouting, in English and in Dutch.

You offered her a raisin and I giggled. She berated and accused me.

"Stop all this now and come with me. You have not completed your own job. This is the day for Inspection. Come and clean your toilets properly," she said.

I bundled you up and grabbed a banana, oatcakes and juice. I threw nappies into a bag and I put your wellies on your feet. I had no idea that I had sole responsibility for the hygiene in the bunkhouse. I already have enough to take care of. She accuses me of trying to ruin her business. We jog after her and she leads me to the problem.

"This morning, I find all this today. I have not slept and I come in here and I find green slime and mildew." She said.

"Well, if I had some bleach, I could get rid of it." I reply.

There is no such invention here as bleach. Good old fashioned bleach gets rid of mould and mildew in a trice. But I had to ask, had to open my big mouth and ask where the bleach was. And so I am an idiot, unaware of the harm that the simple, effective, cleaning solution can do.

"Harm no living thing," she roars.

She then lists the effects of chemicals on the environment, and she rants and she yells some more. Now, here I am with some vinegar and lemon and secret herb or flower concoction and a nail brush and an assortment of old vests. I am scrubbing the individual bathroom tiles, around the toilets and around the showers and halfway up the walls and across the floors. There are three bathrooms and four shower rooms. I have been allotted thirty minutes for each of them. She is in the communal kitchen, which is a little way down the hall. I can hear cupboards being emptied and stools dragging across the floor, the whine of steel on slate, the clink of empty beer bottles; the crinkle of a Crisp Rice cereal packet that a guest has left behind.

My wrist aches. I am bored. I do not like the smell of the environmentally correct cleaning solution. I dip the brush in the bowl and scrub a patch, rinse the area and then rub it dry with a rag. And yes, it shines and, of course, the gloop is gone. I started in one corner of this shower cubicle and I have inched my way along the skirting board and under the heated towel rail and into the shower tray and over to the sink, around the sink pedestal and then back to the door. This is only the first room. There are six more. My knees hurt. I think of my Mother and her tales of Catholic girls in the west of Ireland always on their knees praying. I wonder what my Mother used to pray for and whether she ever got what she wanted. I wonder if she prayed for a handsome man with a good job to come along and take her away from the bog. If so, she got what she wanted but it didn't make her happy. I wonder what I could pray for. Could I, should I pray for the opportunity to see, to speak with my Mother? I scrub and I wonder.

You are giggling outside. There is a baby goat kicking her heels in the yard. It seems you have made a pal. The door at the bottom of the hall is open and I can see out to the gardens. Summer sunlight, warm and tempting may be my prize as it shines at the end of my task. Past the row of doors, dark in comparison, the morning beams into this gloomy corridor. A tantalising reward awaits me: the daylight, balmy and bright, and a happy, chuckling child, an incentive for industry. I switch hands, put the cloth, someone's discarded underwear, in my other hand and begin anew, aim the stitching into the grout and with hard, tight, motions I concentrate on the job, and rinse, wipe and polish. Now that I have identified a goal it seems easier. I can peer around the door and down the dim passage to the radiance of the day; can imagine the afternoon activities you and I may do on this rare, glorious day – soon as I have cleaned seven rooms.

"Mother?" A querying shout comes up the stairs at the back of the communal kitchen. I have not seen Wallace for a fortnight, not since I ran away into the wood the day after he babysat, and since he lost his temper with me. There has been not one word or sign from him since he launched that attack on me. I was waiting for an apology, but I am learning too that he doesn't say sorry. He has come in through the main house and up the back stairs that adjoin the bunkhouse. She barks a reply in Dutch.

"I want a conversation with you Mother, a normal conversation. We live in Scotland, Ma, won't you speak in English, and stop letting on you can't understand me," he said. His voice is loud.

"You, you come now with full moons and half moons just to bring another test for me. Already I am pushed to my limit. This day the Inspector is to come to see my place and maybe I get stars for brochure and free advertising. You have your own business, why you not out stealing money from Americans?" she asked.

"Oh Ma, you're wasting away here when you should clearly be up on the stage making folk hee-haw with all your funny ways," he said.

He sounds like he is sneering, sarcasm and anger coiled, ready to be unleashed.

"What you want, son?" she asked.

"…A favour. And I know it'll be hard for you, but I'm going to ask and then I'm going to insist. And then I'm going to make absolutely sure you do as I ask," he says.

There is a crash, the sound of crockery being thrown into a sink.

"You can ask, son. If it is the right thing, then the Universe will provide for you. If this favour is in the interests of Highest Good then I will do it with no problems, and if I cannot do this thing, I will tell you why and I will help you to understand that the world does not do what you want it do to, but that you must help the Universe instead."

"Mary thinks she was talking with owls. She came back from your full moon meditation acting odd. This is your fault. She'll never handle all that stuff you do. Don't go getting her involved in your weird nonsense. Please, Mother."

The sarcasm intensifies. I know the way he curls his lip. He really is going to blame me. Maybe he already does. Maybe he thinks I made him lose his temper.

"It is my job here on this planet to open the minds of the people, you know this," she said.

"I want you to leave Mary out of it," he replied. "I haven't seen her for two weeks and the last time I saw her she was acting strangely, her eyes were glassy and she couldn't function properly. And, Mother, she was talking about owls and she was trying to think what they were saying. She thought she had been speaking with birds."

Disdainful, arrogant egotist meets his nemesis: his mother.

"Well, she journeyed to meet her Power Animal, maybe: is good. It means she have Guides to help her. Means maybe she start on journey of the Soul: is not a problem. No problem at all."

The owls. I had forgotten. I was trying to remember what they said.

"Will you quit all this mumbo-jumbo. This is the woman I want to marry. I don't want her all messed up with your crap," he replied.

I am on to my second toilet. I am on my knees scrubbing the gunk of years from my potential Mother in Law's guests' bathrooms. I am polishing and perfecting porcelain pedestals that paying guests may piss in spotless pans. I am falling. I am floating. I can hear you play. You are safe, you cannot hear this terrible tantrum; you must not be exposed to the wickedness adults display when hurt. I can hear them scream and shout at each other in the kitchen. This is their normal. Insults are fired back and forth. Voices rise. Tempers flare. Doors bang. Feet stomp. He is pacing up and down through the kitchen, kicking out at the rubbish and the furniture. He leaves the room and crashes the door, comes in again, banging again. He tells her how mad she is, how weird she is, how awful a Mother she is. My eyes lose focus.

"My beautiful son, I do not understand why it is that I cannot help you? So very many people come to me to learn the ways of the soul, and to clear their auras and their energies, but you do not learn, not even one thing from me. This woman you say you love, she is lost. She only know she want to be Mother. She does not know who she is or what else life may have for her. She has not come to me because you want child. She come to learn about the journey of the soul."

"Ma, will you ever change the record? This is all I've ever heard out of you and it's plain rubbish. You want to help all these other folk to be as fucking crazy as you. And I can tell you why and all – that way, if there's more folk all believing the same shite you do then you're justified in leaving your kids. That's all that this is about. You can admit it now. Go on. I'm a grown man, and I can take it. Tell me you just never wanted to be a Mother. You were just too selfish, couldn't handle all the sacrifices; could not cope with the workload. You just wanted to toke all day and hang with all the cool Amsterdam artists. There's no shame now, you know. The Dam in the sixties, I'd would have gone off my head and all. But don't go leading Mary into all that. Her soul is just fine and doesn't need you to be tampering with it. She does not need to get sucked into the spirit world or the way of the shaman or return to her past lives to heal anything. Her wee kid needs her just the way she is. And I need them both. So leave them alone."

A violent silence covered the kitchen and crept out into the hall, down to where I crouched on the floor staring into a shower tray circled with mildew. A stunned Gertrude let into the angry air a long, lonely sigh. A triumphant son waited, ready for the backlash, hungry for a fight, desperate for the chance to tell his Mother how he felt when she abandoned him.

Now I remember the owls. I conjure them into my imagination. I speak to them, as if they were here in the bathrooms. I unload my grief and sadness into the emptiness. I whinge at the mildew, pretending it is a fantastical feathered beast.

I want my Mother. My heart yearns for her care, her love, and her attention. The father of my child has run away, and will not love his daughter, and this strange man wants her, wants total control of her and he says he loves me. But I know he does not, and I am useless and I need help to raise her. I do not know what the right thing to do is, and I think I have made a mistake and his mother is mad at me – and I can't even clean toilets properly. I have no money, and I live in a caravan. I have lost everything, my house; my parents, my job. We do not even have a television any more. Now I am living a lie in order to please someone, anyone. It is not working. I do not love this man but if I stay with him then maybe, someday, I'll have a house but I'll always have to be grateful to him and do what he says. I think he's damaged by something his mother did, and what I really want is for my Angel to know her own Granny. I need to remember where I came from, her strength and her beauty are inside me and I cannot reach them, cannot find myself. I am lost."

It comes in a gush. The torrent of troubles spills out onto the tiles. My voice is a whine – it has not the strength of adult conviction but the toneless pleadings of a child.

I had no idea that I felt this way. But there's my story circling me like the fungus on the shower tray, and almost as colourful.

I just want you to be loved, small, beautiful child. I want everyone to love you as I do. I want your Granny to stop trying to be young, free and single and to show love to another generation. I would like the strength to contact her, I know she would come. I would like to visit my Father and have him recognise me, see you as one of his own. I want your stupid, errant Dad to stop gallivanting and grow up and show love instead of hate.

I am helpless. I am stuck here between two warring nations, their histories and their agendas vying for control of you and me. I cannot force my parents to give me the house in Fortingall. I am stuck here, and I may have to marry Wallace. If I marry him, then I will have the force of his hurt directed at me. He is hurt. He is damaged; it must escape from his body somehow. I will be his next target, and you will learn to be a victim. I must change. I must learn.

Wallace and Gertrude are still arguing. I go into the kitchen. She is tearing at her clothes; pulling at her apron then shaking both hands in the air. She is screaming some sort of nonsense. He is banging his fist on a table. If I tolerate this, then you will surely have to, too.

"I can hear you arguing about me. I have been cleaning. Your shouting, your tantrums can be heard all over the house. Thank God Angel has not heard you. I do not wish to listen to all that. It is awful. Only I will decide who I marry and whether my soul is in need of salvation. Now, come and help me get these rooms spotless."

6

THE BOTHER WITH BENEFITS

The Minch lies quietly today. Fishing boats patrol its length; gannets dive perpendicular into its expanse, submerge themselves completely in its bounty, and surface again, their beaks full. Early morning mists rise between the whin and the bramble. The hedges are smoking.

Gertrude's eyes are cloudy, cataracts forming, the fog of age demanding milk bottle specs, and the best excuse to smoke grass. Her chair has a long straight back and she presses herself into it, rubbing a little, ironing out the bed-tensions. She leans into it, hunches forward. There's always a crack of tension stuck somewhere in her shoulders, a niggled knot of muscle unwilling to yield to yoga. She thinks a Pilates class for Grannies may be a sound business venture. She loves this chair, this ritual of stretching.

She has hidden a stone in a brown paper bag. She needs her stone, this rock that she has kept here for half a year. It came from Orkney and it is ideal, the perfect pumice. Yesterday's flakes of dry skin fall out of the bag as the stone emerges. Gertrude sighs and moans as she lifts her foot to her lap, and grates the stone along her heel, grinding it into the ball of her foot. The wrinkles and layers of skin move. Bits of her drop into the cracks in the wooden floorboards.

Scraps from saris have been made into soft furnishings for this room, silks for cushions and curtains. She stripped the old leaded paint from the floor and the door when she was younger, when she still had the energy for such things. Goats' milk sours in jars on a shelf. Sour goats' milk is the best stuff for shining brass door knobs or an old institution clock.

She is suddenly shamed and reddens. She realises we have been watching, waiting. Her huge, naked feet, with varicose veins and bunions in abundance are all we can see.

"This is my own space," she barks at us. Her tongue seems not to work correctly, "You must in music room wait for me."

You stare at her feet and look terribly worried. Gertrude tries to smile, but it is only a strangled attempt at a smile and you run to her and put your arms around her.

"It be ok Gert', not worry, have some my hugs," you say.

Her fierce heart softens, we can see it in her eyes, and she accepts the little act of love from my child.

We go into the music room. The other woman is in there, Gertrude's constant companion. She is sitting quietly, staring out of the window. The small, fat one is called Elsie. She is English, but fluent in many languages. She never says much but we always feel her thinking, as if she has great thoughts to keep her occupied and so cannot really spare the time for small talk.

Gertrude comes in and Elsie gets up and crosses the room to greet her. Elsie reaches as high as she can and strokes the older woman's face, draws her lips to her own, and kisses her wholly on the mouth, looking into her greying eyes. Gertrude nods gently, sighs and asks for coffee. The small round woman wanders off. Gertrude comes to join us. My jaw had dropped near out of its socket as they kissed. The open intimacy of it, as if seeing her feet had not been enough of a shock. The sight of the two women displaying their love and sexuality has stunned me. I have seen two women kissing before. I have kissed a girl. It was a long time ago, and it brought me many troubles. Her lips were sweeter than Wallace's.

Elsie returns. My ears and eyes are fixed on their every word and every activity. There has been some trouble with one of the local crofters, some dispute about boundaries and grazing rights, and she is fed up. Elsie tries to comfort her but Gertrude directs her fury at me, mistaking my shock at her actions for interest in her problems.

"These old men think I am witch. Think my friends all witches. I tell him that whisky no good for him, it put out his lights and make his dick soft. I tell him to eat good food and have piss in a jar, keep piss to rub into flaky, nasty rash of dandruff on scalp. I tell him the very best cure for that disgusting stuff that come off his head. He did just look at me strange. I am old woman, much older than he. I know these things. I have drunk my piss for many years now and my skin is very fine. I am wise. He came to tell me we must marry. He come with cheap whisky and tell me to have a dram. I can drink more, much more than he, but I do not need to. He say he need me to be drunk so he can kiss me.

"I have kiss many men and now have no interest in them. I tell him I am lousy selfish woman in bed, like to talk about my heart and about all my feelings in the day. I too old to fuck now. I tell him his dick maybe too soft and there is not enough Viagra in all world to make him hard. He think I know all cures for his dick and that I fix him up good. He says he have much land and I have much land and we should marry and be very rich. Mary, maybe you marry this man and then he not bother me and

I show you how to make him so tired he just sleep all the time, and one day he not wake at all and you and Angel be rich. Maybe you think about it".

I want to leave the room and go and laugh somewhere. I have come to the big house today because she has promised to take us to town. I have not come for voyeurism or intrusion into their private lives or for some arranged marriage to a smelly, impotent old crofter with terminal dandruff – and I certainly did not arrive here this day to watch Gertie slough the scales off her old soles.

Elsie makes great coffee; prepares peppermint tea for you. We sit and sup. Gertrude seethes. I stare at the statue of the Goddess and wonder where I have seen this thing before. It is the model of a tall, elegant woman in a flowing robe with a flower in her hand. I know it from somewhere. You wander over to the piano and plink and play. You see the African drums and you tap your little palms on the skin. You rattle a rainmaker. Gertrude relaxes a little. My small, beautiful child, you can touch the universal Mother in even the most weathered of bodies. She is still and peaceful for a moment. She smiles over at me. You return to the piano, ping the high notes. She has a sad smile.

"I left my children. You know this now. I left them with their Grand Mother. Vall and his sister. I did not see them grow. I thought I had more important things to do than be a Mother. When I bought this piano I thought I would see them play it. But they were then too grown for this kind of little exploring of the music of the world. It is my very great sadness. Vall not tell you, I think. He does not understand; only see he was left with no Mamma. I came here to this island because it was the right thing for me at that time. It is very long story and about my past life and I will tell for you another time. I wanted to bring my children but there was never the right time. Now, one hates me and I do not know where de other is. His name not Wallace you know; his name Walter. He tell lies to suit himself, not aware of his truth."

All the revelations of the morning have kept my jaw locked down in shock. Her brogue baffles me. My understanding is limited. I do not question her.

"You know that is hard to be Mother, but still you carry on. I think you are very strong woman. It is good now that you have owl to guide you."

There really is nothing for me to say. I nod and smile. I watch you having fun. We drink the coffee and she gets up and declares that she must change her clothes in order to go to town. You and I sit at the piano in this lovely light filled room and we make music and you finish your peppermint tea. You eat a couple of oat cakes and then a banana and half an apple. I realise you do not need to be breastfed so often now and the thought makes me relieved, though a little sad. I wonder if Elsie has children. I wonder if they fell in love with each other, these two women, whether they had longings for the intimacies of their own sex or whether they got so fed up and disappointed with men that it was just a natural progression?

Gertrude enters the room again. She has a dress on. There are thin blue pinstripes running the length of it, her swollen ankles peek out the bottom and her great feet are now housed in yellow, wooden clogs. Over the dress is an apron, a red and blue embroidered tabard with flowers on its sash. She has a necktie to match, a shawl in similar reds and on her head a large floating white boat. The hat has wings; starched edges like a nun's head dress. Traditional dress I presume. I am beginning to understand Wallace and his ways.

It is a two hour drive to the main town, the largest village, and I sit in the front seat of her car. You sit in the baby seat in the back and fall asleep. I watch the scenery and the sheep and the stone walls and the buzzards perched on fences. I am captive, held by her babblings. I feign interest. I examine the needle-work on her costume. I think of Wallace and only really listen when she speaks of him. Mostly, she speaks of her own history with the island and the great works she and her pals are achieving.

"There were not so many foreigners here when I first came. There were just the native Islanders. Maybe some from other islands. But all had been on their own here for a very long, long time. They had been trying to survive, and it was hard. They bring children into the world and not know what will happen, will there be enough food, what will happen if someone gets sick or if Pappa drown at sea. Where will the children go after school? There was no work here, no college, nothing. When I came, there were other women also, other families from other places. The locals call us the 'White Settler'. You know this; they call us still this name.

Gertrude and Elsie had husbands and children but discard-ed them, left all that life for the sake of a dream. Kith and kin were forsaken for boggy tracts of land and sweet solitude. Acres of poor land demanded their attentions. Their focus is the earth. Their devotion to Mother Earth is their vocation. They know the old ways and yet they see far into the future. They want to heal the hurt of this island and there are dozens like her. It is the hidden corners that home these folk, the re-mote crofts and corries, the far-flung heather-homes of fey folk from history and imagination. They dream together of drainage systems, of ways to replace the rushes and bog myrtle with apple trees and willow beds. To plant and grow, to reap and sow, to clear the blockages the mining made. Hairy, overweight women at odds with their men and disappointed with their children, have found passion here, together.

Gertrude preaches about the material world and its evils. She reprimands all shoppers and all consumers. She lauds the frugal and the thrifty. She says the food chain is poisoned by chemicals. There is something wrong with wheat and with cows, I am not exactly sure what, but I think I may know more by the end of this day. She believes that chemical companies thrive on our illnesses and thus the economy grows. The Government controls us by compromising our immune systems. She says we are all sedated by bad food, antibiotics and immunisations. We have been lulled into semi-consciousness by the distractions of designer labels and celebrity. We work and we work so that we may have money and we spend and we spend that money and then we must go back to work. And of course she has the answer, the panacea, the cure for all this. We must purge and we must cleanse the decades of disease from our bodies and our genes. With herbs, with homeopathy, with home grown food we can achieve perfection.

The skills of the wise women of long ago still flourish in the minds of Gertrude's friends and peers. It is their vision for the future, that we leave greed and over-indulgence and embrace each other in peace and love. The answer is simple, is simplicity itself. Knowledge has been gathered from around the world, researched and adapted and one outcome of it all. We already have enough. We already have everything we need.

"But you want Daddy for little one. Yes? You think my son

will make good Daddy? Oh no, I do not think so. I think you have many lessons to learn and that my son will try to control you. He has no respect for woman. This is my fault, of course. He is a small, hurt child who will have a tantrum any time he does not get what he wants. Also, he is lazy. He will not help you unless you find a way to make him. Also, he steals what he wants, takes from what he sees around him; never ever repays his debts. You do not need him. I knew you before you were pregnant. Often I would visit my friend and she was your neighbour. Many of us gathered there at her house for full moon and new moon celebrations. She has gone now, to Wales. We had meditations on Mondays and some special days. You remember her? She had a beautiful statue in her garden and you used to walk past with the dog and admire it? Yes, it is the one of the Goddess that is now in my music room. I used to see you because we put our piss into the garden and so, often I vas pissing in the potatoes and looking into your vegetable patch. I wanted to tell you about ways to fertilise your own soil and maybe then your strawberries would not have been so disappointing."

I look sideways at her. She knows she has my full attention now. She smirks and I realise she has been waiting to have this talk with me.

"You two were just so handsome together. We see you out fucking sometimes. So happy, and so free and so full of love and passion for each other. All my friends talked about you both. There was no one who could see you two married. We could detect the glint in your eye even from a distance, we knew, we knew that you would never settle for this man. Any man. We see you when we pray for good harvest. We wanted stall in the village at market. We wanted to show all the crofters what big cucumbers we had. We grew carrots and courgettes. We wanted to show them all what would happen if the land was loved and fertilised naturally and with no chemicals. Oh, yes, we prayed and we danced for fertility. We sang and we connected to Mother Earth. We asked our Guides for help. We weeded and we planted crystals and we pleaded. And we watched you with your cans of Glyphosate, trying to kill the Japanese Knotweed and we saw you rolling around with your man.

"You were such a child and we spoke about you all the time. We knew it would not last. You were so very beautiful and independent and clever. But he just wanted to boast that he could fuck you. We knew; when you sprayed with the Round Up that something terrible would happen. You must not hurt the land. He left you then, when you tell him about the baby. I remember you. I remember all you girls got pregnant. There were eighteen of you got babies that year. And just all around the house of my friend. We think this because of all the dancing we do. We think that this is our doing. The harvest was fantastic that year too. We think that we make the land bear fruit and we think we make the people fruitful also."

We are in town now. She stops the car, switches off the engine and you wake as though from a hypnotised state, bleary eyed and bewildered. I feel bewildered myself. My brain seems to be coated in a liquid; swims around unfettered to anything, and this fluid has affected my ability to see. It runs out of my eyes because it has nowhere else to go. And so my cheeks are sodden and I cannot tend to you because I cannot function on any level, and so she must take you and hold you and comfort you and there is nothing, nothing at all I can do about it.

Gertrude strides into the supermarket, clumping along in

clogs, and you try to grab the tips of her bonnet.

The supermarket's loud speakers sing suicide, narcotics and rehab. The chart-topper leaves her pain over the bread and the morning rolls. Elderly crofters and ancient wifies can make no sense of it. Someone in an office somewhere has dreamed up this scheme: confuse them at the door; blast them with strange sounds and threats of death. It'll work wonders in the Highlands of Scotland. The think-tank thinks blast chart music on the days the buses bring the country folk into town for their weekly shop, and classical music when the teenagers are in after school, so that they may have peace.

Bright lights warm the tops of heads. Stale air with fish and sheep and cows in it moves into lungs. I stand next to Gertrude. You run up and down the rows of captured vegetables. I hold a packet of courgettes. I want to touch their hard green skin. The wrapping is a hindrance to my senses. I prepare to open it, see if they grew in this incubator or whether they hold any scent of soil. You find sweeties with ease. There is a stream of shelves, low rows with neatly segregated, pretty coloured packets – pinks for girls and blues for boys. A larder of frozen sandwiches stands next to the sweets, and the base shelf has bottles of fizz and pop just within reach of a toddler. You want the neon one, the glowing red juice, and you know instinctively how to get it

"I tirsty Mamma. I wanna dink Mamma."

Which version of 'no' will suffice?

The drama is inevitable. You have seen something you want. Now I must buy it or suffer the consequences. Bottles of water are almost hidden in a corner of the larder. They are less than one pound each and twice the price of the bottled bubbles, but I reach for one.

"Oooh, look at this one, this is a magic one. This is invisible, just like fairy nectar. That other stuff must be for trolls," I say, and lead you away from the poison. You fall for it, and I hoist you into the trolley. Instant gratification is the necessity of the child, so I open the cap and let you suck at the bottle. I do not care if others think I am stealing. I have averted a war. I am happy. I lean over and kiss you, reward you and help you forget the sugar drops.

"Good girl. You gonna help Mamma find bananas?" The sing-song voice always distracts you. I use it often.

"Let's count bananas. One. Five. Two. What's next?"

"Gertie want some my dink? It make you a fairy."

Gertrude is locked in battle with a man, a fisherman by the smell of him. Her passion for the debate is obvious. He's having fun.

"This is Tom the Pipe. He is the fisherman supposed to bring prawns. This is Mary, she stay with me just now."

I am introduced to the beer belly first. It is as round as a medicine ball.

"There's no more prawns," he says.

"I tell you twenty year ago. I say if you fish all the time then there will be none left."

"And is it a medal now you're after for being the clever one?"

There is a notion of tobacco coming off him, and fish scales are embedded under his fingernails. He baits her. She changes the subject.

"Mary has this beautiful child. But the Daddy has no love and no money to give the little one. They have been all alone."

He enjoys his game, returns to where his knowledge lies, comes again to the sea.

"And 'tis thirty year I've been out on yon boat, ever since the day after I left school. I've seen the salmon go but never did I believe the prawns would dry up."

She can't resist the reiteration.

"But I tell you. I absolutely tell you. It is fresh still in my mind. I come down the pier as your boat come in and I see all the creels and I watch you two times in the day fill all they pots and I say to you not to send all the food to Spain. I say you must take only what you need. I tell to the driver of the van not to take all the fish, tell him he stupid. I speak with all the men on all the boats teach what the old Indian know. I tell you what happen to greed".

He loves it. He just wants her to speak with him. The memory is still in his mind, the day the huge Dutch woman came down the jetty as the boat docked. He remembers her clogs, looks at her feet and smiles, recalls the first time he saw her in this rig-out. She spent years coming down to the boats. She was like an old whore or fish wife, except she never went with any of his men. She just lectured them. She was the precursor of the government fishing quotas. He looks around and winks at his pals, at anyone he knows even vaguely. He'll have something to say over a pint and a dram tonight – 'guess who I was chatting up in the Co-Op?' – he can foretell the responses of his drinking buddies: 'She hasn't had a man for all the time she's been here, yer in there boy, oh yer in there.'

She turns her body so that I am the central focus. Both pairs of eyes wait for me to speak. He notices me now. Breasts first. Then my size sixteen body. I get the impression he would like to examine my teeth, then turn me around so he could squeeze my ass, test it for firmness. He has a very raw sensuality, the way beasts do. I'll give him something to gossip about.

I pull out one of the caged courgettes. I put the wrapper

down. I simper and move my head to one side, flick a little hair away from my face. I make my eyes big and bring the tuber up to my nose, pretending to sniff. I stroke it.

"Do you grow any veg?" I ask.

He's surprised that I speak. He's probably surprised any woman speaks.

"No. It's my brother got the croft. He has those things I think."

I run my fingers up and down its hard bulbous head. I bring my eyes up to him and then back down. He follows my gaze. I flicker my eyelashes, twice.

"This one smells funny" I say. I bring it up again, let it linger under my nose and then lick my lips repeatedly. I sigh, deeply. I moan and caress it carefully. I have his attention.

"I love fresh vegetables."

I turn to Gertrude. I lean in to her.

"I suppose we'd better hurry up in here if we want to get all the jobs done today. I have an appointment at the benefits office."

He's left alone in the aisle. The beer belly covers any possible indiscretion. Gertrude is quiet. She cannot confront me.

We mingle. I stay close to her for protection. You sit for seconds at a stretch. The corridor of cakes and biscuits was a revelation for you. Your podgy arms swung around in the air and your legs drummed against mine, each swing slightly more vicious until I relented and released you from the confines of the trolley. This was a mistake, of course. I should have endured the beating of your feet on my thigh and the direct hits into my stomach. 'Stop kicking Mamma', did not work. I had thought it might. 'Little feet, stop kicking', had absolutely no impact. I let you out.

'No!' was ignored. 'No opening the biccies, baby. Ah ah! Leave those alone', and so for what seemed like an age I scolded and nagged and sweated. Shiny automatons of domesticity and virtue, dreary housewives, shook heads and tutted.

"They beat children. This one can explore the world. Is good for her to see all these things. Look at these other children, have no spirit, have to be on best behaviour all of the time. Is not good".

You are darting from shelf to shelf, shaking and crinkling cartons. This is not your usual morning nature walk. This is new and exciting. I reach out to grab you but you evade recapture. The inside of my head is heating up and chaos looms. I will rue the day, I know I will. It is the wrong thing to do, but I do it anyway. I take a box of iced biscuits and display them to you.

"Come up now for Mammy and be a good girl, Mammy give you biccies, come on, up, up and sit nice." I say.

There's no other way. I have no time to play today. I sit you back in the seat and give you what you wanted. I relax. My body cools. A little voice, sounding a whole lot like my Mother, scorns me, offers platitudes and clichés endorsing a different method of motherhood.

I try to emulate my peers. I attempt a veneer of purity. But it's really a Sara Lee double chocolate chip gateau I hanker after, the dark brown ooze that so softly melts on the tongue. It has not yet occurred to me that they are all wishing for the same thing, for various combinations of fags, booze and chocolate cake.

There are two queues from two tills. The only male in the store has a procession which tapers through the candles and light bulbs. A shorter, fatter line shuffles from the bored wee lassie to the shortbread. It seems to me that those having trouble with their gall bladders have been separated from their leaner sisters. The obese ones chant silently to the fresh-faced, slim slip of a thing. As each fatty hands over the weekly budget she joins the mantra. Each individual thinks as one. Many women, one thought – some day you'll look like this is their bitter whisper.

And she scans and pings under hairy chins and rolls of fat and deep, deep down in the recesses of her grey matter she hears them, over and over again, day after day, and week after week. She used to fight it, used to don make up and add a jaunty little scarf. Now she deems it inevitable: furry upper lips; rings embedded in swelled up joints, an ever-present sneer. She believes them now. Life holds no mystery.

I remain by Gertrude. The air is thick with gossip and I know I will have my thirty seconds of slagging-off later in several houses and cafes. Going about with this foreign oddity is bound to provoke discussion in even the most charitable of dwellings. We do not need to flirt with the token man. We stand and wait for the wee lassie. I feed you biscuits, a pink donut. And here she is, like a bloodhound.

"Hiya Mary, we've not laid eyes on you for weeks. Oh! Hasn't the wee one grown? Is Mummy letting you at the junk food now? Are ya still seeing that gorgeous fella with the kilt? I do catch him in the village the odd time but he's always alone."

I've forgotten her name but can recall her troop of darling boys. She sweeps our stuff through her scanner. We pack it in cotton bags.

"This is his Mother." It is a boast, plain and simple. "I live out on her croft, out past the piping museum. He's very busy of course, building his business, he's doing ever so well, getting bookings on the new website from all over the world. And he's got tons of ideas." I smile and gloat.

She smiles at Gertrude. "I love your outfit, where did ya get it?"

Gertrude is stern-faced and serious about such issues.

"It is national dress of Nederland"

"Oh, that's near Holland, isn't it? And your son wears the old national dress of Scotland – must be a family thing? That'll be seventy eight pounds and eighty pence please."

Gertrude hands over cash. She waits for a receipt and then we walk toward the door, leaving the sound system still playing inappropriate noises to the elderly.

We stare at each other. I note a question in her eyes. Gert is puzzled. She crumples her brows and scratches at a wart on the side of her nose.

"Yes, I had not ever thought about dat. Vall, he want to dress up to be like me, I think this now."

I am shocked it's taken her this long to understand. He is her progeny, he has learned her habits; he emulates her in order to gain her acceptance. But I do not wish to elaborate, do not wish to disclose my role as confidant to both parties. Distraction techniques are the forte of Mothers.

"You've known that fisherman for a long time, then?"

She is sharp and can compartmentalise the uneasy thoughts regarding her one and only son quite succinctly. She has done this for many years now, file maternal feelings. We put the bags in her car.

"Oh, yes. I like fish, you see. So, I go to the fishing and I see how it all works and I think all raiding of the sea would not happen if the Native American ruled the world. Or if any of these people here listen to de words of the Native American – they had so very much wisdom you see."

There is still a quiver over her brow. One eye has a glazed look. She's thinking again.

"That Fisherman is very rich. He has never had a wife. His family has much land. They have many sheep, cows and lots of land for houses. He has a very big house and his brother, also without wife, has a large mansion – all that money, and no woman or child to spend it on, is not so good. He actually has two boats you know, that mean he pay two crew. It might be good idea to see if we can match you. He take care of the little Angel. My son is no good for marriage, he have too many problems. I think now it is good, better with the fisher than the idiot."

This is not the place for a showdown about Wallace. I ignore her. I have walked around this awful shop with this madwoman as though she were my Mother-in law. I have endured her delusional diatribes since just after dawn. I have fended off the lecherous lump that she now wants to marry me off to. Wallace needs to talk to her. It isn't my place. But it could be so simple. All I would have to say is why do you put him down? Why do you not like your son? Why did you not raise him? Why do you show him indifference instead of love? But I cannot. Not here anyway. Not in the Co-op car park. Now I want to hold him. But I have an appointment and must hurry to the job centre.

JobCentrePlus. The Benefits Office to those of us who frequent it. I have been invited here today for an interview. It is normal practice. Mothers must be questioned and then reminded that merely mothering is not viable for the economy. One must work, gain wages and spend. Those are the rules of our society. You race around. Gert has to sit with the great island unwashed. I know she is fearful of nits, fleas and scabies.

I know she will be breathing in to her aura and saying spells for protection from all transmitted beasties and diseases. You find forms and take them. You find a pen. I catch you seconds before you begin drawing on the walls. I have a large brown envelope with my details: my six months of bank statements; the photo-copied application forms for income support and housing benefit, dated six months ago; letter from child benefit office; letter from the Child Support Agency confirming I have actively pursued the child's Father for maintenance but that he is non-compliant, that they await a deductions from earnings order. Also, from Gertrude, the rent book, unpaid for two months now and of course the file with all the Council Tax demands. Everyone here has a bundle of Council Tax demands that they cannot pay.

"Mrs MacKinnon?"

"Miss." It is a declaration of stature, of strength.

"Come with me, please. Your daughter can come too. I have a pink marker she can play with."

A faint, internal alarm sounds as we go into an office. I had watched the others being interrogated right here in front of me, sitting at those desks. I am not sure why we are being led into a private space. I look at Gertie, but she is deep in another dimension, focused only on sending messages of love and respect to all the crawling creatures that in all probability dwell in and on her immediate neighbour, but urging them not to abandon their comfortable home to explore her body.

"Have you brought the requested documentation?"

"Yes."

"Thank you. I'll take them and photocopy them, you can stay here and fill in these forms".

You clamber on to my knee and hang your arms about my

neck. She leaves. I begin the forms. There is a shuttered and mirrored window just beyond the desk. I wonder if there is a two way mirror with a camera hidden behind it. I fill in claim forms, for housing benefit and council tax relief. There is another one for child tax credits, but I ignore it, positive that I won't qualify.

"You are in arrears with your rent." She has returned.

"Yes. I have already submitted twice but I have no confirmation that my requests have even been considered." This is my posh, educated voice, the one I used long ago.

"You have been refused housing benefit." She remains calm, disdainful, snooty. I get the impression this is her source of power. I imagine she has a violent husband that she cannot control or leave, and she needs this job for a sense of self-importance.

"Why?" Dare I question her obvious authority?

"You appear to have made yourself intentionally homeless."

"No, I haven't." I am without any sense of this. I have absolutely no idea what she might mean. I want to cry. Gertrude is out there hoping for a large cheque as back-payment in rent. Please God she doesn't pick up anything from the guy next to her.

"Let me explain, MISS MacKinnon. You were awarded a new house, were you not?"

I can say yes, I know I can, mouth open now and speak.

"You were awarded housing benefit for that property and also Council Tax Benefit. The Government has already provided accommodation, free accommodation. For you and your child, Miss MacKinnon, a new house, on a new development, many others would have liked that house, local people would have liked that house, but you wanted to live elsewhere. You did not request a transfer. You did not inform the council of your intention to vacate the property. You did not follow procedure. Therefore you did not abide by the rules of the tenancy agreement. And yet you approach the public purse for more money, more benefits."

She is frightening.

"I note from your bank statements that you have been in receipt of incapacity benefit. Previous to your income support claim you actually had more money coming in than the law says you need to live on. And yet, did you contribute to taxes or water rates? No. Miss MacKinnon, you have in effect, defrauded the Government."

She pauses for dramatic effect, and possibly also for breath. I am overwhelmed. I thought this was a mere power hungry country fool with no education and an unhappy marriage, but I was wrong. This is the sacred guardian of the State coffers. She is the representative of the Chancellor of the Exchequer and protects the finances of Scotland from the likes of me.

"I have invited you here today to allow you an opportunity to appeal against our decision, to inform us of your options. I understand from your paperwork that you currently reside in a caravan. I presume this is a ploy so that you may attempt to apply for another council house at some stage. I have reason to believe that your application is false, as you stay with your partner's Mother. We find it rather unusual, and unbelievable that a Mother would choose to live in a caravan rather than in a new built house in a scheme designed especially for lone parents and their children. In light of this, I have asked one of the social workers to visit you, at this alleged caravan, to inspect what else may be happening out there, to ascertain if it is indeed where you live and whether it is suitable for a child."

A piece of my brain shuts down. I sort of lose consciousness. I enter a dream state. High above the village, higher than the mountains, hidden by the clouds is a large platform. The top is flat, flatter than a bowling green. I am there now. I raise my sword. My opponent raises hers. We each fight for that in which we believe. Images are displayed on a large screen. They are our thoughts and fears. We clash. She has the work ethic emblazoned on her breast. The family unit is her trump card, the bastion of the bible and normality. I slash her ideals with the obstacles of life and show her my own poor paralysed Daddy, your confused Daddy, my relatives far far away. She charges now with full force laying all blame at my feet and ready to kill me in retribution for not caring for my parents or my lovers. I am weak. The steel beats the armour on my shoulder and the duel seems over, with each blow she cries in triumph. I cannot be a good mother if I beg for benefit, abandon my family and refuse to marry the father of my child. The point is nearly home. I concede.

Almost, but I have another illustration in my defence. I display the scheme built especially for lone parents: the patches of dirt for the children to play on; the used condoms already there in the mornings; the syringes left where they fell from veins; the ends of joints and matches ready to be tried; the stolen bags and purses thrown behind the only bush; the stack of car stereos the Police couldn't find; the crowbar used in the break-in on the shinty club; the desperation in dozens of hearts in search of an exit. She is a noble Treasurer. I am an outcast on the brink of society. On the edge of a society already condemned and maligned. I lay down the sword and with head in hands I declare that I have held a job, I have contributed to the economy, I was a beautician, I paid taxes, once. I tell her I was ill, claimed Incapacity, that I am better, that the Incapacity was stopped almost half a year ago. She relents. She backs away and leaves me to stand and gain composure.

I hear Gertrude. I hear her shouting. You whimper and whinge in my arms. We are in the grey room. Gert is outside in the waiting area. I drifted off again. Did I speak? Have I explained my situation to the interviewer? Perhaps I just sat here in silence and said nothing, looking vacant and bewildered? Help me, someone, please. I offer up a prayer. My shoulders are sore and I feel like Atlas, with all the world of worries on my back. If I cannot pay her rent, she will ask me to leave. I have nowhere to go. My benefit has been stopped. I have no other money. She is screaming out there, something about pity. She is asking them to pity me. Oh dear God. The underdog, she exclaims. She thinks the Scottish prefer to be kept squashed down. This is her perfect situation, her soap-box dream. The original anarchist invites grey men and doormat women to rise up and fight. But no one in living memory has ever held down a job, nurtured a career, expected. This is the benefits culture and there is no way she can comprehend it. Third generation dole queue and everyone a sinner, does not lend itself to self-esteem, self improvement, self. She may rant. They cannot hear.

I grab her and shush her and bid her sit. I look at the only woman in the room with a job and a husband and a mortgage and three kids kitted out from the Next catalogue.

"I'll file an appeal," I say. Gertrude breathes again, the same way my Mother used to, through her nose in slow, deep inhalations, down to the tips of her toes and then out in a rush from her mouth. I copy her. I breathe Light. I send Love to what I cannot understand. I make a mental note to contact my own Mother.

7

FREE LOVE

The bellies of mussel shells shine. Their backs broken by a bird
– the curlew maybe – sharp daggers made of their houses.
Their insides cleaned and gleaming on the side of the rock. The
dog scents a recently departed otter and her nostrils bang and
her tail beats, and she jogs up and down the shore. A lone, returning goose honks overhead. Me and my brew are outside,
balanced on a log.

You are inside now, stretched from one end of the double bed
to the other. Your dolls and teddies are snuggled beside you.
I relish the dawn, these dreeping mornings of dewy grasses,
the shouting and fighting of sea birds. I have one hour. I treasure it.

In my lap is a school exercise book. I am writing my appeal.
I am trying to recall all the reasons why I ran out of Drumlie
Dub, and list them in some sort of order. I have fourteen days to
submit this work. I may have to appear before a panel of adjudi-
cators. I am nervous but can show neither you nor Gertrude my
anguish. I fear she may get involved again, start a campaign in
favour of poor dispossessed single mothers on benefit; become
the voice for a people she does not know or understand. I have
promised to weed and dig today, spread manure and seaweed.

I am working twice as hard now, trying to compensate for the lack of rent money. Sometimes, I feel she takes advantage of my vulnerability and other times I feel she is kind and I am in her debt. I am unsure of the true situation. But still I say nothing, for fear of offending.

The oyster catcher family is feuding. Their high, shrill peeps are everywhere. Late lambs jump together. I knew my view could improve. I used to gaze into the living room of the house opposite me in Drumlie Dub, and in my heart I knew I could find a way out. I knew there was better, beyond. Every day I dreamed and every day I prayed to be offered sanctuary. Now I must compose a letter to a departmental delegate to explain why I found the affordable housing scheme so intolerable that I ran away to live in a caravan with no inside toilet. It may be a long letter. Of course, I knew there were procedures and protocols for grievances and complaints against noise and the like. I read about anti-social behaviour orders. But with no back-up, with no family or partner, no true pal to speak with me or defend me I would have exposed us to a danger I could not quantify. I was afraid to openly criticize. Tomorrow morning I shall pretend to be an oyster catcher and squawk and shriek to the water and the woods. For one more day I will listen and learn what I can of the world.

The tide has left a line of kelp high on the shore. Sticks jut out. Rubbish from boats seems to drift in for a time and then out again. A heron waits, like a grey brush stroke, at the edge of the water.

Wallace will be here tonight. I must wash. I must boil water in a big pot on the gas ring and fill a basin. Or jump in a river. The grooming of the mane is the most tedious task and sometimes I yearn for a shower, for the small comforts of modern living – they have been sacrificed for the sake of safety and sanity. And I could not return, will not ever now swap gadgets, trappings, taps and tanks of hot water. Not if it was detrimental to the finely tuned harmonies of my soul. Forever may I stay on this log, just above the water. This is the stuff I am made of: the moons and tides and the echo of the ocean – not the discombobulated boredom of a Scottish housing scheme, even if stretching out in a tub of hot bubbles is the rightful reward to every woman at the close of her day. Now, what to tell the woman in the office?

I will wash later, when the work is done for this day, when the kelp is lifted and spread on the bean rows, when you are weary and in need of a nap. When we come back down to our beach shelter I'll sit and shape the brows. I'll devise some method for shaving my legs and my under arms. He likes to know we are here, waiting for him, dependant on him, reliant on his tales and adventures from out there in the world.

I refill my coffee. I stare at you, your rounded cheeks and innocent bliss. You look like one of those out-doorsy kids from magazines, with earth grooved into your fingers. The window in our bedroom is steamed up. The cardboard-like walls are peeling. Moulds and mildew ruin clothes in cupboards. But I have not seen a police car out here.

As though you had one ear trained to respond to the kettle, you wake as it clicks off. I fill my cafetiere and then sit with my arms open for you, for your early morning warmth. Dazed, and newly returned from your dream time you need to accustom your senses to a new day. We do that with cuddles. I have no energy for battles and already you are free to choose what to wear. I bring breakfast outside in an old ice cream tub, fruit and bread and juice, to be nibbled or sipped as required. I know

I must enforce some sort of discipline soon, structure you so that if your Granny should ever deign to visit, she won't be totally appalled at our lack of social graces. It is wrong to say she would be appalled; if I gave her half a chance, she would grab you with open arms, hold you tight, lightly berate me for the way I am. She would try to fix the things she could. She could teach you how to dance, some day. But that day may never come and so, let us go out and dig and catch wiggly worms and I'll teach you a song I know.

I avoid the house this morning. I know what Gertrude wants me to do. An old carpet has been left to rot on a corner at the bottom of the garden. The creeping buttercup underneath should, in theory, be almost dead. I give you a spade and an old biscuit tin. You bang and bash the ground. Your banana is dipped in dirt then eaten. I take a hefty spade and stamp it into the earth all around the old carpet. It has decayed. A wood louse clambers away to darkness. Bits of it come away at a time. The once fine fibres are smeared in slime. It smells of deep places. A robin comes to see what we are doing. She seems to think she is a supervisor and directs me to dig here or over there, where there may be worms. When I find one, I hand it to you, sing a worm song; you in turn hand it over to the robin, and teach her a tune about her snack. You insist on cleaning them before she eats them. With a wet wipe you swab one and place it in front of our bossy little friend. She keeps you entertained. She is possibly the best babysitter I have ever known. The clay is heavy; many years of rubble have been deposited here. Roof slates, bits of china and stone and stone and more stone. I am crouched there all the morning, clearing roots and rocks while you wash worms.

The earth is turned over. The kelp is spread. I stink. You are filthy. We walk back to the big house with the feathered one following.

"They're very friendly with fairies," I say. "When a baby fairy is tiny, she doesn't know how to fly. Just like you. You didn't know how to fly when you were born, or to walk. The robins are a great help to the fairy Mammies. In their red chests they have a secret hidey hole. They put the baby fairy in there when the Mammy is flying around collecting teeth or nectar."

You are rapt.

"Cos the baby might fall off the Mammy fairy's back. Remember when she was singing and she made a big balloon in her throat? Well, when she does that, then the fairy can press it and the magic door opens so the wee little one can be popped in to the warm soft pocket and be all cosy and safe. She can even pop her head out and look around. And, the robin stays close to the Mammy fairy, so that the baby can always see her Mammy if she wants."

You have renewed respect for robins. The bird follows us. When we reach the house we take off our muddy wellies. We hear voices in the music room. You run to find Gertrude. I take some bread from the kitchen and crumple it on the outside of the window sill.

"Thank you for minding my daughter," I say, "please come back tomorrow. We live in the caravan down where the river meets the loch. We will find more food. We think you are very beautiful. We love your singing."

I go in, wash my hands and then go to see what's happening.

There are forty or so women and men in the room, mostly women. Every Wise Woman in the Western Isles is here. There has been a call to arms, or maybe, wands. I recognise some of them as guests in the bunkhouse. I had not realised at the time that so-and-so was Wicca. There's the one who leaves sherry in tiny crystal glasses out for the little creatures at the bottom of her croft. I find you, bring you over to talk to her.

"A baby fairy was in my robin," you tell her.

She kneels on the floor and wraps both her arms around you. She declares, most sincerely:

"Oh, that is most magically fabby-dooby-doo."

You hug her back. You seem delighted to have a conspirator other than your mother, who is probably dull and unreliable anyway. She has several purple silk scarves wrapped around her. She gives you one to dress up in. "Look Mum. We are like twins."

There is one main conversation. Some local landowner has been granted planning permission on one of their sacred sites. They are not happy. Elsie has called everyone here to participate in a sacred ceremony. They are going to protect an ancient portal. I am invited. I am bundled into a skirt. Everyone, even the men, have to wear skirts for ceremonies. Your new silk scarf is fashioned into a toga. Beads are added. You are presented with a long thin rose quartz.

"The little ones are the wisest. They are still in tune with the world. She already feels the power in this, don't you, little one?"

"I have some small pebbles from Iona, give her these, see how she reacts".

"Later. There's no time now. I'll let her keep that one. Look, she likes it. Does it tingle in your hand?"

We are instructed to eat and I take some lumps of banana bread and refill the ice cream tub. Some home made goat's cheese, chocolate brownies (I sniff in case there's any grass in them, but I don't detect any) and molasses flapjacks; homemade quiche; salad and a fork and spoon. I even fill a flask with a mixture of camomile and peppermint tea. I wonder about Wallace; should I leave him a note? No, we'll be back soon. I don't know anything about portals or ceremonies. But it beats trying to shave my legs while standing in a bucket of tepid water.

We are taken in a car. There is an ancient cathedral on a small island in the middle of a river. Elsie offers the history of the place. She even sings a bit, telling us Mairi Mhor, one of the great voices here, often mentioned this place in song. Many battles have been fought. It is said the river once ran red with blood. We stand on an old stone bridge and watch fierce water rush from the mountains in its hurry to reach the sea. Hazel trees thrive, although on one flank, the tops have been roughly sawn, levelled. You and I and our dog walk down a path. The dozen or so cars in our company park along the old single track road. Cows look up in surprise. Tea is being made. Crystals are discussed. Intentions coded. A splinter group – rebels, perhaps – sit in a circle and meditate.

"The energies are so light here."

"Yes, I agree, I can feel my higher chakras resonating."

"There are many from Spirit here, many who have gone to the Light."

The dog finds a low place to paddle. We join her. Blackthorn trees weep mint-green tangles. Orange willows spindle. The sun glints on the water and the tentacles dip into forgotten bricks. The dog picks out rocks. There is a picnic bench. I leave our shoes and socks there. We hop on rocks, we dip our feet. I have one eye trained on you, the other on the action.

A series of stepping stones tempts some of them.

"We'll need to clear any negative energy from the burial sites."

"Ask the Ancestors for help."

"We can cross here."

All the coloured silks of the world wave pouches with secret herbs and energised rocks. In open toe sandals they hop over the churning foam to dry land. One pulls a large candle from his bag. He lights it. They begin a chant. There is an elm tree in the centre of The Island of the Dead. It is here they stand; their violet drapes clash with the lush green grass. They jar against ancient dry stone dykes. The grass is luminous over there, possibly because of all the decomposed bodies fertilising the soil. There are crypts and cairns. A tarnished bronze plate honours the Bishops of the Isles. Images of Vikings are carved into marble and slate, great swords etched forever between their legs.

"Ancestors, we ask you for your help!" A male voice is raised.

The entire assembly stretches out behind the decapitated trees and down the lane. They rim the proposed building site. I cannot hear them over the river's roar. I can see their faces, blank and serene. I can smell the burning sage. You and I eat banana bread. I wait for the climax, but it never comes. Some arms are raised and objects are buried all around. No smoke, no mysterious visitors. I feed you quiche. The sun goes down. A monstrous yellow moon takes to the sky. Now I hear them. They whoop and howl. We sip tea. I eat the chocolate brownies and give you the iron-rich date and walnut flapjack, in case of cannabis. They dance and sing and chant. We watch as though television was just being invented before us. One by one they leave their positions. It is custom, it seems, to bow low to the ground, placing both palms together as though in prayer. Hands sweep over spaces beyond bodies. I finish the salad. I pack up our belongings.

"Show's over, Ange."

"Wha' they doo-ing, Mamma?"

"They dancing. But time for bed now."

"Why?"

They are invigorated, happy. The deed is done.

"I felt the change, did you?"

"No one will ever be happy to live there."

"The house will not be built."

"The spirit of the trees is healed now."

"We have closed the gate. No more can come through this way."

At home, Wallace is livid. He has been waiting. His chin is thrust forward and his top lip is high and tight. Eyes narrowed, arms plastered into his chest, white knuckles displayed, he reminds me of my Father. The displeasure he feels is initially directed at our outfits, as though our first crime was to go out in anything other than the attire he has meticulously chosen. One arm is thrust out so that he can run his fingertips along the fabric of my skirt and subsequently snort at it. I try to see as he sees – this grubby wild pair bedecked in hippy cast-offs have replaced the manufactured mannequins I had been attempting to imitate – and I offer him my humble, apologetic side. He removes your grubby scarf and hands it to its original owner. We watch the nostrils flare. He looks like a man in need of a stiff dram. I take your hand. I take his hand. We leave. Gertrude has a silent, satisfied air. As she bends to kiss you goodnight she checks that the rose quartz wand remains hidden in your pocket. She winks at me. Her son casts all his demons into one look and directs it at her, but she ignores him.

I simper next to him. I become submissive. I do not challenge his bad mood. I flirt. I whisper offers of sex in his ear. I tell him

I love him. I run my hand along his back, softly, then with a little force, a little touch of fingernail. I thrust my thumb into the muscles of his shoulders, rubbing and sighing and helping him change his mood again. The darkness lifts from him. He can feel powerful in his thoughts of sex. He feels better thinking how he could take me later. He probably won't, but I know he likes to think he could.

It is the first night he has spent in the caravan. The three of us sleep together with the dog pawing the bedroom floor. He has left his pack by the door again, ever ready should a quick getaway be required. In the morning he hands me an emerald knee length skirt – my size, a charity shop find. It is beautiful and I am grateful. Also in the man-bag is a new pair of patent black leather shoes for you. This has become a regular pattern and I am now unsure whether it can be allowed to continue. Maybe we can travel with him. Next time I could choose our own clothes.

"The bus is free today. I am as free as a bird this fine sunny, Sunday morn. And I have a plan. Got wheels. Got time. Got the weather. Wanna surprise Angel? Wanna come out for the day, the pair of ye?"

He is happy. Maybe still thinking about how to take me and show me what a great man and lover he is. I will flirt some more later. I prefer this mood of his.

The little robin is perched out on my washing line. She has a pal and they are singing. I search for scraps to scatter. She comes and takes them, returns to gently drop the bits into the other beak. A fatter version of herself with a slow, stupid look, I presume this is the last of her chicks to fledge.

"Go on and get yourself sorted out, Mary. I hope you don't mind me saying, but your hair's needing some conditioner or something. You're not looking your best, sister."

"I'll run up to the showers at the bunkhouse if you'll mind Angie."

"Sure, off you go."

The bunkhouse is quiet. It seems empty. I lean into hot steam. Dirty trickles swirl into the plughole. I scrape stubs of fingernails into my scalp, releasing furrows of dust. It is the thing I miss. Yes, secretly I desire a power shower in a fully equipped wet room. Maybe I could find a way to create something similar here.

I want it all. Finally I understand the human craving for Utopia, the very personal pieces of Heaven we each think we need. I smother my body in cream. I return through the main house. It is also silent. They are all at morning meditation, wrapped in their rainbows, squatting on small orange cushions in her Peace House. All their energy centres aligned after a day and a night loving and protecting the planet. I would like to be there.

When I return to the caravan, coffee is made and you are scrubbed. You are adorable in a cotton dress with shiny shoes. I am tempted to put a bow in your hair. He is shaving. A towel knotted about his waist, I am treated to the toned chest with perfect abs, the hunks of arms: the hunk of man. I wrap my arms about the girth of him, rest my cheek on the taut muscle of his back. Gently run my mouth along his naked chest. Taste him.

"Get off me woman, you're soaking me."

"Where are we going?" I don't think he's likely to tell me, but I ask anyway.

"You were not hearing me last night, now, were you? If you had been, you'd know now. I'm not happy about all that shite me Ma goes on about. It's no good for the wee wain. I know.

I had to put up with all that when I was a lad."

Oh no, not again. It is true. I was not listening to him last night. I was relaxed and sleepy and it was bliss to hold him in bed. I let my mind wander, forgot to pay attention to reality.

"We're going to the Kirk"

It is an announcement, the order of a dictator. This new, kinder, mood has not sprung from some deep desire for my sexual advances – he has plotted a different type of power to wield.

"Your wee one needs me. Last night her teeny wee hand was wrapped around just one of my big fingers. You were drooling on me other shoulder. And the smell off the both of ye wasn't good. I don't think you've washed your bodies since the last time I was here. It's bogging. Me Ma is off her head an' so's all her pals. You cannot be letting this Angel here rot and go ga-ga with they maddies. I'll be keeping more of an eye on you. There's more business up here now. I'm gonna show you how to live out here on the back of the island. After all, I brought ye out here and shouldn't have left you dependent on me Mother 'cos I know all too well what she's up to, there's honest sinners at the local Church. There's a Sunday school for herself and you'll need a hat, cover your head."

"Mamma, my robin here. Wa-Wa, come see a baby fairy. Is in the birdie's tummy, see Wa-Wa, see her magic button."

"Just wait now, just hold it a second sweetie, Mamma and Wa-Wa gotta speak."

With that he pulls me by the arm into the bedroom. His face is like a cardiac episode. He hisses in my ear: "This, this is what I'm meaning. Fairies! Ye can't be teaching her of fairies. She'll be hammered in school for less. Think woman, use the sodding brain, what if she came down to Glasgow and she was all filthy dirty and spouting rubbish? She'll never make a pal."

It has nothing to do with you. He's reliving his own trauma. His childhood is fresh in his mind. He is fixing his past through us. I'll go and hold his hand and sit through this service, help him salve a sore knee his Mother never kissed. I'll hide that rose quartz in the box my Pappa made. Glasgow! He might take us to Glasgow.

Tweeds and pleats and black hats, that is what the women wear to Church, plain suits and ties for the men. A greeter at the door grasps wrists, a big man I've met before somewhere, says: "About time too," to Wallace or to me. They shake big paws, and a woman gets the nod to approach. She is eighty, maybe more and her mouth is a thin line of toil. Her eyes are lowered and I can sense the control she has over her tongue. She puts her two arms on your shoulders and guides you away.

"She'll be happy in our Sunday School," he says to Wallace.

We enter. It is high and bare. There are many pews, many empty. I was not prepared. I did not know you would be in another room. I cannot think. I do not know what you are doing, whether there are other children, what will you be taught? Will they tell you fairies are not real? I fret and fidget. Plain voices lilt, bass booming, sonorous psalms. Sinners repent unspeakable deeds. Lamenting the hammer lifted on the Sabbath, the slate that needed knocked back on the roof lest the rain get in; the thirst which nothing but the water of life could quench; the desires of the flesh, all the lapses from the path of Christ. There's no Heavenly choir. They have no musical instrument. They have only their own souls to raise in song. I forget you and remember humanity instead.

Later, after Wallace has gone, you and I admire the drawing you did in Sunday School – two robins and some purple fairies.

8

SACRED SEX

The rufty tufty woof let the stranger in. She probably showed our visitor into our bedroom. Maybe let her tongue stretch to the proffered hand. Maybe licked her in welcome. Probably flapped her ears for tickles, rolled on her belly inviting scratches. The first I knew of the alien was the hot breath panting at my head. The knocking of her tail on the wall. The little cough. My dog does not cough.

I ease out of bed without waking you. I close the door. I put on trousers over the fleecy pyjamas I got from my old aunt in Ireland. It is too early for questions, only time for coffee and a pee, my only concerns.

She is wearing a rainbow striped cardigan. It is bobbly. Her hair is frizzy. She carries a briefcase. The three minute trek through nettles to the compost toilet is not an option, I do not want to leave you alone with an interloper. The food is kept in the bathroom.

"Tea or coffee?" I ask, reaching in the supply and searching for normal tea bags adding: "I hope goat's milk is ok?"

How quickly we adapt.

"Miss MacKinnon, I am from Social Work." She says.

"Sugar?"

I produce the old ice cream tub, there are lumps of banana bread left.

"Please excuse me, I need to pee".

Behind the van I let go, bare my ass and relieve my bladder. Then, looking up, I see two female Police officers. I don't wipe but drip dry in the fleecy jammies with the soft cotton trousers over them.

"Good morning," one said, "I am sorry we are so early. We had a report and we are concerned about you and your child."

"Would you like tea or coffee? Do you mind goat's milk? You won't even taste any difference."

They come in too. The three of them sit on the couch, crushed together in the corner, knees touching under the table. Our knickers dry on a pink plastic pulley just above their heads.

"The child is asleep," Frizz tells Uniform. "They share a bed."

Notebooks are produced, their eyes scan my living space, into my kitchen; the sink and cupboard; one shelf, a long the built-in unit they track, the books we read, the drawings; shells.

"Do you mind if we look around?"

"Sure, go ahead."

The police sit. The social worker wanders about, opens the bathroom door; sees my larder. A drawer displays our entire wardrobes, the half a dozen trousers and T-shirts we own, the new green skirt hung on a hanger over the door. A Tupperware box of socks and pants lives on the shelf in the kitchen next to my dinner service. She twiddles a knob on the gas cooker, lifts the matches to a higher altitude. And there she finds it, an ash tray, a joint sitting in a scallop shell.

The bastard, I think.

"It isn't mine," I say – how trite, how stupid.

"Is there a next of kin for your daughter, nearby?" Frizz asks.

"No."

"Is there anyone to look after her? You may have to come with us for questioning."

"I don't think that is going to be appropriate in this case. Research shows a caution along with education to be highly effective in these situations. Sudden separation from the primary care giver can be detrimental to the welfare of the child."

"Where is her Father?"

"I think he works in the garage, he used to, I don't know. They've never met. That is not my joint. That is my boyfriend's joint. He's made a mistake. I'll tell him, don't worry, I'll tell him. It won't happen again. I promise."

"I think a caution will be satisfactory. Follow up investigation. Sign her for parenting classes. Counselling; see if there's an underlying issue. We'll have to see her in town when you've organised childcare. We'll take a statement then. The Children's Panel has their procedures."

"What do we do about the living accommodation? This is below standard. There's no toilet."

"She's been on the housing list before; moved out here from Drumlie Dub. Gave up a new build house to move here."

"Does this demonstrate putting a child at risk?"

"It could be described as child friendly."

I stare at the smudges of small hands on the smooth of the Formica. Treasures stored in corners; a doll, stones, the cardboard box bus. Outside, Mrs. Bossy Robin demands breakfast.

"She'll be awake in a minute. If you're all here, she'll get frightened."

"I'll stay, chat with her; make sure she's alright. You two can go. I'm sure you have more urgent cases."

She turns to me and curls the corners of her mouth. I know she's going to explain the situation, patronise me a bit and give me a good fright so that she doesn't have to trek out to the back of beyond ever again.

"We had a call from a concerned individual. We understand you were both out very late two nights ago and that the wee one had no coat on. We have been led to believe that you were in the company of some unsavoury characters and that there may have been drugs involved. Would you care to comment? Also, we understand you are experiencing financial difficulties and that the intervention of the Social Work team may be appropriate at this time".

"Yes, we were out. No, no drugs. She had a woolly cardigan and a scarf."

"What support do you have? Have you family nearby? You say there's no contact between you and the child's Father, is there a problem there? You may need to contact him regarding these alleged incidents. We can help with that."

A policewoman finishes her tea and stands up. She touches the elbow of the social worker, scans the van and says she'll be in touch later. The caravan lurches as their weight lingers at the door. The two, shiny blue women leave. The social worker takes off her grubby cardie, hands me her mug, and asks for a refill. We sit and speak. She asks a lot of questions. I cannot listen because it feels like the roof of my head has been blown off.

You wake. Like your Mother, you stumble sleepily into furniture, then my arms. Nappy off, drink in hand, you notice the note-taker.

"See my robin?" You say, "See she's magic button? Is a fairy hiding."

I remind you about your picture. You find it, present it. She praises you and you smile and show the new teeth.

"When was the Health Visitor here last?"

"The Health Visitor has never been here."

"When did you last see her?"

"When I came back from hospital. When she was born."

"But, that must be two years ago, surely you've seen her since?"

"No. There's only one for the whole north end of the island. She can't do everything."

"Have any of her developmental checks been done? Have you had the little red book filled in?"

"No."

"Well, that is the first thing we must do. I shall organise transport and bring you into the medical centre at the hospital. We'll get both of you checked out. I may refer you to some agencies. You have disappeared off our radar for some reason, we will rectify that," she pauses for thought. A blue paper file is opened, she peers at a checklist.

"Is she up to date with her immunisation program?"

"No, she hasn't had any."

The attempt at sincerity evaporates. Her next expression is, at least, genuine. She cannot compose herself. The veneer of professionalism dulls.

"You are responsible for the health of this child, Miss MacKinnon. You must bring her for check-ups. You must."

"She hasn't been sick. She's perfectly healthy." I am experiencing her best bad mother stare and I am not frightened. I am a fool. I know I should shed a tear and declare life to be a tumultuous struggle. I am aware that the correct procedure, when dealing with Social Workers, is to beg for help. So, I don't. I dig a great big hole for myself.

"I breastfed her until a few months ago and, contrary to your initial impression, I do not use drugs or alcohol. I have grown our vegetables and they are organic. We lead a very healthy life and I have not felt vaccinations or antibiotics to be necessary. I don't believe I have done anything illegal. Look at her. Come over here, Angel. Leave Woof alone and come to Mamma."

"Mary – may I call you Mary? Yes? Good. Mary, we have many people and organisations to support you, direct you, keep you on the right path through this difficult time when you are learning how to parent a child."

There is an inflection at the end of some of her words. Her speech is a bit like a song; scaling notes for maximum effect.

"I will have to send a report to the Children's Reporter and a committee will decide what measures need to be taken to prevent this occurring again."

"Prevent what from reoccurring?"

"Prevent me from visiting you again, for instance. Maybe you are pleased to see me? Do you have any company out here?"

"As far as I can tell, some mean-minded idiot has sent you out here out of boredom or malice. You have responded to a nuisance call. You should check your records to see who your informant is."

"The manager of the benefits office contacted me, actually, and I had a delay in responding, so when the second call came in I was alarmed and came as soon as I could. I don't have to disclose this. I shouldn't. I just want you to know. People are worried about you. Do you have difficulty accepting that? Do you think people should not care about you?"

I simply do not believe her. I sit you on my knee and tickle your ears, beep your nose and ignore her.

She is skilled, knows her time is up and prepares her departure speech. I do not listen. She does not interact with you and I think nothing of it.

She goes but she leaves tension behind, and I chomp angrily at my porridge. Then I march us out into the woods but I find no relief there and we trek up the hill, past the hand painted signs advertising accommodation and holistic massage; goats with heavy udders and the bee hives.

Gertrude is in the kitchen. She is making cheese. The air is sour. I add my acquired bitterness.

"Oh Vall, not again. Stupid boy. He did this all the time when he was small. Every time I have some joints he phone for my Mother. No. He not do that now. He is grown man now, not a silly boy trying to get attention. No, he has changed. Sorry, I should not have mentioned it. There will be another explanation. Maybe some neighbour, sometime they can do that here. I have many stories about people who have not fitted in so well with locals and island peoples call Authorities for so small tings. One very silly man did call police one time when he found a very tiny scratch on the side of his van. I remember this, I think at the time that maybe his penis was no good at all and that is why he had to worry so much about his van."

This is her way. The only empathetic technique she has ever really learned, to recount her own experiences and, by doing so, offer a conspiratorial bond. She will continue in this manner for the day, perhaps the entire week. Until another topic comes to distract her from the current one. All I wanted was a hug. Her memories allow me sanctuary from my own situation. I stay and we play. We prepare bread and watch cheese being made. She talks.

I know he did it. I see his game as he has seen mine. He is going to undermine me in the only real place he can. By exposing me as a bad Mother, he can draw attention to his own Mother's faults and failures. He has forgotten one crucial detail. I had a good one. I know what I am doing. I was taught by my Mother and she was wonderful. Her strength and integrity flows through these veins. She fought my Father and his society in order to raise me the way she did. I will follow in her footsteps. He cannot harm us.

I don't feel afraid. But I nod and agree. I have lived in Drumlie Dub. A neighbour once held a knife to his daughter's throat. Another was a regular tag-wearer, in and out of jail. I am familiar with the police; know they will do nothing. If there is fear, it stems from that striped, frizzed woman who stood at the foot of my bed this very morning and watched as the drool dripped from my slung open mouth. They take children, I know they do. I have heard my old neighbours from the cities talking about the kids in care, the nieces and nephews living away from their parents. It is the whispered word; revered like cancer; Social Worker.

"I did not choose to come here. Not to this Scottish Island. I was sent here. The Guides told me that I must come and show the people here a different way. It is my destiny to help these islanders evolve. I have many skills to raise consciousness of people. Twenty five years experience healing pains in hearts and all blockages and old hurts. I help you release fears."

Oh dear, what is she going to show me now? Last week, it was some sort of enema. The week before, she told me to take a piss in the vegetable patch. Before she tampers with my mind I should ask to see a certificate. There's training, professional hypnotists. Which University did she attend to learn to peer into my mind? But she was right about the meditation – it is calming. And the brown rice diet certainly took all the baby fat off me. And I could use a little distraction.

"I know to hypnotise and then take you back in time to different lives you have lived. You see hurts, problems and then you heal them. I help. We look to find out your lessons and after you can move on with your life. We just send love into dark places, kiss and make better – like I see you do with little one."

It sounds easy.

"Come, we ask Elsie to sit with Angel. We go to the Chamber. Do a Healing."

I nod and follow.

Yellow flag irises inject sun; golden gorse balances charred black earth. Ritual burnings of heath and field leave soil naked, scorched and exposed. The neighbouring farmer annually annihilates new heather growth with fire. Not Gertrude, no, she doesn't torch her meadow. I have seen her lying in the buttercups asking them to grow and fill the world with their beauty, and then urinating on them, to help them along. Maybe that is why we must giant-step through them now; lift our legs high over the monster-stalks. The roof of the meditation chamber is also yellow. It is a good meal for one goat.

She introduces me to the room. She lights candles with dedications to healing – the healing of me! We sit low. She wraps a rug around her shoulders and flicks a bedraggled feather at me. She counts, and I prepare to sleep.

I am in a garden. Tall hedges have been shaped ornately. Women in hoops and petticoats decorate a lawn. Men in high hats sip tea from china cups. A white horse behind a white picket fence attracts me. I go to the horse and a large door frame appears. In my hand I have a key and through it I go.

There are cobbles underfoot. I hear her voice questioning.

"What is on your feet?" She asks, and when I think of them they hurt, my toes are pinched into long grey boats. I scratch my chin because my beard itches. I am a banker and I am in a hurry to meet my partner. We are embezzling money from two establishments. I have come from the house of my employer. We had lunch. He hinted at discrepancies in my accounts. I panicked, and smothered him with a bolster from the chaise longue. All this I know and feel and see. I am alive in this place but my body is in the turf-roofed garden shed. Gertrude asks questions and the images come. But, she wants me back in this world and it has been too short and I would like to stay and look around and see the past. The pictures in my mind are prettier than my reality. But return I must, and I do reluctantly.

And now I endure her analysis. The theory about my asthma and my lack of money. From whence it came. She will return me to that time and place but the moon must be full or new and I must be made ready to accept the healing from the other planes. My mind is to be focused first, and she knows just how to do it. Solstice is in two days time and to celebrate she has invited the bunkhouse guests and all her pals to walk on hot coals, and now, I am to join them. From all this I will manifest abundance and the financial struggle will cease. The Salbutamol inhaler may be binned, or, preferably, recycled, and her fee is one hundred and twenty pounds, please.

The answers to the mysteries of my existence spew forth. She compares my meagre karma with her own great cosmic debt. As penance or divine retribution for the sin of murder by suffocation, I have chosen asthma so that I may learn. She, on the other hand, had been a great and wealthy landowner in these parts many centuries ago, and had sport torturing peasants and shooting deer.

"When I first came to the island, I was very proud. I had a good education and I had travelled and seen much of world. Quickly I discover I am being superior to the Scots and they do not like this at all. I understand humility here. It is the realization of many people who choose to live here. I think settlers come here to meet with this island must bow down to the mountains asking kindly to have notions of grandeur taken away painlessly. I see too many lowered to ground because of fanciful desires or ideas. This is no place for ego."

This woman stomps and glowers her way through every day of the week. Her word is law. Her suggestions and pieces of advice are orders. Her business is run as a dictatorship. There is no energy wasted on the non-compliant; Wallace for instance. I do not want to think about the person she was before she learned humility and respect for the less well-educated. If life is, as she says, a series of lessons, then she really must be due one major shock. Or, Wallace may be correct: she's mad.

"You must celebrate Solstice with us. You may ask goddess to help clean your past and in ceremony ask for blessings. Tomorrow we start making shelter for the sweat lodge. You will help.

* * *

A dome, a cave we built by bending willow. A team of woman in wellingtons and midge repellent shaped it and tied it with hemp. I helped. You helped. The dog attracted midges and demanded all of the sticks. The fire pit was dug early this morning. The wood pile was stacked nearby. When the frame was built, old worn towels were thrown over it and then a blue plastic sheet over that. The covering makes it seem apart from the meadow and the fire. It feels safe, secure, yet earthy, like a burrow or a mole hill. We were sent away with sideways glances. We were asked to gather flowers for the consecration ceremony. This is the sweat lodge. It is dedicated to the Goddess. Large, round, smooth stones were placed in the fire, herbal unguents were scattered as wishes were revealed.

"I wish to shed this skin, and fly with friend Eagle," said the lady with the purple scarves.

"I wish for World Peace," said one with brightly patterned boots.

The stones are still in there. They glow red and umber. Fools' Gold sparks. We will walk on them tonight. A little breeze catches some smoke and brushes it into the air. My eyes follow the haze, note the drift. We are late. We made daisy chains and decorated you with them. We stayed and played in the wild meadow with the bog cotton and the peats already cut. You model our afternoon's activity, a tiara and garlands, a buttercup bangle. We have returned with lilies, purple and yellow.

The sound from the bender brings me again to the present. You run with the dog, and stop. There is music playing. You peer in. The dog stands at the door. You are both quiet. Your attention is focused, and held by something inside. You do not notice me stand beside you. One voice lilts the lyrics of Sufi or Sappho – easy rhymes and rhythmic meter. I poke my head around the corner of the door.

Tea lights twinkle. A lyre lifts the dust from the floor. The dozen women who built this dome are kneeling down. They are robed. Their eyes are shut. They face, not inwards, but outwards. They have formed a semi-circle. Something moves in the centre, but their backs are turned to it, as though not wishing to see. Another pit of hot stones sizzles in the corner. Fragrances spill out of the cave. I detect myrrh and rose. You hold your nose. The dog sneezes.

We should go, but we cannot. We are rooted here. You watch the swaying of cloth, the gilded embroidery in shiny satins. You scan the serene faces. The lady who gave you the crystal wand is here, crouched on the floor with her arms by her sides, palms facing out, eyes shut, meditating.

Two figures lie on the floor. Sheltered by the robes their feet seem bound at the soles. Their legs are entwined and their bare chests heave in harmony. Through smoke and steam some pubic hair fizzles greyly. A woman I do not know stands over them; she dangles a dousing crystal, balancing their chakras. She is also the singer. She reminds me of the Rock Folk. Gertrude and Elsie trace fingers into each others' cellulite. A fat arm cups the still-firm breast opposite. A toned bicep stretches to a saggy sack. Four thick dark nipples poke their way into the candlelight.

The couple let low moans escape. They unfurl their legs. They breathe together, staring deeply into one another's eyes, trance-like. Each has a hand in the other's crotch. Their fine pincer movements resemble the picking and plucking of the lyre strings. The female standing passes a small pottery jar to them. The swell of her breast rises then points through her thin cotton top. There is no quest in her, unlike the others, searching for miracles and meaning. She practises the rituals with reverence but is detached from this crowd. She slides silky hands into a runny, gelatinous fluid. The woman wears a white gypsy top, a white skirt, her feet are bare. She is the daughter, the sister, she is beautiful. The oil is applied to shoulders, necks, breasts, stomachs, groins; smeared and shiny; soaked and set. Water is thrown on the stones, herbs and petals sprinkled, pungent preparations added. She passes a dildo. It looks like it was found on an archaeological dig. The women raise their voices now. An oscillating rhythm controls the cave. You move close to me and hide your face and peek out again and I gather you in and turn your shoulders and click at the dog. I turn my body but keep my face trained inside. I cannot look away. I want to see more. I am not disgusted or shocked, but interested. I do not know what is to happen, and I would love to stay and see; take part, even. But you, you should not see this. There is more education here than I can cope with just now. Gertrude has just strapped the ancient device around her and raised her arms. Antlers from a stag are handed to her, and are fastened to her head. She looks like she should be entombed in a pyramid. They sing a melodic meter. I make my brain concentrate on Wallace. His sister intrudes into my thoughts. I imagine role play. But the dildo is on me. I leave because I do not wish to be caught spying, and because I want to join in far, far, too much.

"Mamma, what they doin?"

It had to happen. You will question this new experience until it is fully understood. There are no answers. Distraction techniques must be employed again. Daisy chains admired, new ones offered.

"I seed Gertie. She did have no pants on. I seed she's hairy bum."

"C'mon you with your daisies and buttercups. C'mon and let's put these poor lilies in water. Mamma is going out later on. You are having a babysitter. Babysitters read lots of stories and make popcorn before night-nights."

We three walk together but in our minds we are far apart. Each of us tries to make sense of the scene just witnessed. We know we have intruded into some other private world. We were voyeurs on a clandestine activity. We feel unsure, as though returning may be an option, another minute perhaps, no one would have noticed. We could have, should have stayed. The nanny goat bleats and charges at the dog. But even the dog is oblivious. Her eyes are glazed blue. She carries the stick now like it is an encumbrance, rather than the prize she ran and ran for most of this afternoon. Her eyes are bleary. The various aromas have affected us, I assume.

The Kitchen Angel watches us take off your shoes and put them on the shelf. She stands hand on hip. She is American and is here in Scotland for six months. She is tracing her ancestry.

"How y'all now? You're not looking good. Little pale. Had a shock?"

We just gape at her.

"Hey, come on in and have some bread. It's good and grounding. Bring you back to earth. Then ye can tell me all about it."

She sweeps us into the kitchen, sits us at the counter on stools and passes a wholemeal loaf with mushroom pate. Numbly we eat.

"Do you like stories? I found some great books. I just love reading to little kids. I make all the voices of all the people. You gotta favourite story? We could make one up. Mama's going to learn a new trick, gonna meet some fun people and get in touch with herself."

She turns to me now, this self-appointed culinary divinity. Her eyes have stored much of the knowledge of the world – another well-travelled independent woman. I am intimidated and envious. She senses my unease. She tries to soften her approach.

"You'll feel good after. I've done it, thought about the instructors' course, but this trip came up. It's good. Makes you feel invincible. Even seen it done in India. Such a powerful medicine."

My big, open, stupidly honest face displays my curiosity, an invitation for her to continue to try and impress me with her studies and experiences.

"I am happy to feed all the people here, prepare the banquet and babysit because I don't wanna get involved down there. This is lots different to what I'm used to. Out in rural India, fire walking is a community event, not a bunch of Ladies keeping things secret. In a month I'm gonna go to the Callanish stones on Lewis for a vision quest. There's a Native American Chief coming over for it to celebrate the visions of shamanic people in different countries. It'll be great. You should come. You can help out in the kitchen or holding the space or maybe you'll be called to dance."

"What's a vision quest?" Stupid woman, I've no filter between thought and speech. Be quiet. Leave now. Get out when there's just a bad taste in your mouth. There may be trouble ahead. But I don't listen to my internal voice. Any attempt my heart, my soul, my intuition has made to keep me safe has been repressed for many years. I think a man will save me. Foolish. So, she has me.

"There are many reasons for a vision quest. The end result is to connect with Spirit and realise the true self. The Natives had many ways. These have been interpreted for white men. Fasting and dancing, calling to Spirit to come and give a vision; a way into the other realms; a way to see a little of your soul; a tool to let go of the damaged past. Many reasons. You may be a dancer. Sit with it. Before you came into this incarnation you made a contract detailing the lessons you were to learn and how this was to be achieved. You're a big girl, could be you'd hold the space well while dancers drift into other realities."

I want to dance. I want it now: sounds fun, sounds interesting. When I left Drumlie Dub I wanted to find a different way. Well, this is it.

"Hey, me and this little cutie'll get better acquainted, you go and hang with the fire walkers".

Go back? Down there? Sure.

"Thanks. See you later" and I go, forget to kiss you.

Will they be finished? What will I have missed?

The dog stays with you. I jog down the single track road. I hop over potholes. Smoke sways from the holy fire. My sight is trained on the spot. They are out. The women have taken off their robes and sit on hunkers and little rocks in the plain work clothes from earlier. There is no orgy, and I am disappointed. My wildest fantasies were about to be realised. I imagined nakedness and writhing. I had eagerly anticipated it.

"Hi, Mary, Come and join us. We have just stopped now. We have had a ceremony inviting Goddess to come into us and guide us. It was good. Some of Her energies will be hanging around, sit and absorb the feelings."

They nod. Reach for each other. Smile and skim skin on skin. Affirm a mutual sense of purpose. They are electrified, happy. They are bound together now by the secret. They will not speak of it with me. I will not disclose my intrusion. We share something. And I have a reason to smile.

"You look so much more relaxed without the wee one. They're just finishing up inside and then we'll begin the Lodge. You'll need to lose some clothes. It gets very hot in there. Have some water just now. How's the wee one getting on with her babysitter?"

"Yes, she seems just lovely. They'll be fine. What do you

mean I should take off my clothes?"

Discreet snorts, vibrations in the back of throats. Big laughs stifled.

"Oh no dear, don't worry. You can keep all your clothes on if you wish. Did no one say? Oh, she may have had other things on her mind. We have towels, T-shirts and shorts. It's a bit like a sauna, hot and steamy."

The crystal dangler stands, wraps a blanket around the figures emerging from the shelter. They leave. I am left alone in this crowd of strangers. I am bemused, expectant and unsure, and also very horny. One pours a line of flour on the ground. She catches me staring and explains it is a barrier – to keep energies separate. It runs from the main fire into the small pit in the centre of the sweat lodge. Sage is smudged over heads, down backs and along the soles of feet. One by one we enter. The crystal dangler returns and adds wood to the fire. The stones from inside are handed to her. She places them back in the flames, separates them from the others. I hear them call her 'Fire Keeper'. Cross-legged we sit in the darkness. The flap has been closed over. No one can view this.

"We shall state our intentions. Share now your spirit name and your reason to be here this evening."

"I am Pale Blue Water. I have lived almost sixty summers. I wish to cleanse my aura; it has been damaged by the life chosen."

I know her. She makes wooden frames from driftwood.

"My name in Spirit is Purple Shadow. I have come here today to embrace the essence of woman, rise up in my own power with the aid of Goddess. I feel so useless in my life. I know there's more out there. I want to learn more about the different cultures of the world; how other women survive all the struggles in their lives and how the ancient ways empowered woman."

I know her too. She runs the village Post Office. I have heard her barking orders at the post man, and seen him take a nip from a thin silver flask. I've seen her eldest girl down by the river with a carry out of cans of strong cider. I think the daughter's pregnant; dropped out of school, anyway.

"I am Wind In The Trees. I am on a spiritual journey into the depths of my soul. I am learning to control my mind".

Oh dear god it's my turn soon, what do I say, no one told me about this.

"My name is Mary. I want to be strong and not have to rely on men, show my daughter that women can be strong and independent. But I don't know how. I thought this might be a good place to start. I used to be a beautician, you see, and now I'm just a single mother on benefit, living in a caravan and I've got the Social Workers and the Police after me and I've no money. My Dad has had a stroke and my Mother's on a cruise and my wee girl's Father has no interest in her. My boyfriend is away a lot and he smokes too much grass, and I think I am living a lie. I just want the opportunity to see my Mother."

On either side they reach out and stroke me, touch my hair, my arm, big sympathy-eyes.

A smoking rock is passed in on a shovel.

"Hot stone! Hot Stone! Incoming! Hot Stone!" And the flap is down again. A little heat is generated. I notice a carving on a plaque. A gruesome female with her breasts exposed and her hand in her vagina – a Sheelagh-na-gig, banned in Ireland, and probably banned here, too.

The flap lifts again – "Hot Stone!"

…And again and again and again. Now it is getting quite

warm. Water is sprinkled on the stones. Steam rises, stings my eyes. Sweat pours out of me. I am a river. The ground underneath me becomes damp from the water dripping down me.

The flap lifts: "Hot Stone!"

"We will chant now for new beginnings. In the Native American culture, simple vowel sounds were given individual meanings. We chant now and offer this to the Spirits of the Four Directions, to come to us now, here in this place and join with Goddess and aid us on our spiritual path, that we may overcome the burdens and train our minds to not only walk bravely on hot coals, but to always walk tall and strong and brave through our lives; to accept with grace all the lessons we have chosen to learn."

"Hot Stone!"

There's no air left in here. It is sweltering. I am in a microwave. I am being cooked. Get me out. Get me out. I take off my fleece. I don't want to, but I have to. I take off my shoes, socks, jeans. That's better. I can barely see because of the thick air and the water running into my eyes. I understand now; she was being kind when she said I should lose some clothes. These women are hardy. They breathe into it, sit still, chant and breathe.

"Hot Stone!"

I try it too. Just force the steam into my nose and down to my lungs, press it into my stomach and down through my legs and then let it slowly back out through my mouth. Count and suck, blow, over and over. I ask the Goddess to help me be a strong woman, deal with the Police and the Social Worker, figure out the benefits system. And then the tears come. Sadness wells up inside me as I think of you; the first time I met you as you were lifted out of me and dropped on my breast to suckle. I think of the shock of having sole responsibility for your tiny life, abandoned by your Father and Grand Parents. Now I am angry. I think of your Father and his fine words and suddenly I want to hurt him – because he will not love you. I sob and shake and the others chant the vowel sounds and sob and shake too. We admit life is tough. We say we hurt. Ask for help. Cry.

It is over. Coming back out again is like re-birth. Surfacing from the pit of dark thoughts into the thin light is disorientating. I shiver. I am handed a slightly used damp towel and the kindness is touching. She smiles and reaches out and calls me sister. She gives me water to drink.

Clothed and rehydrated we go to the Chamber. Arrows are distributed. Long red weapons for shooting and killing, we must snap them using the power of our minds. The point is placed in the hollow of our throats and the feathered end balanced against a hard board. We must step forward and break the arrow. Either we live or we die. I choose to concentrate on the mid-point of the shaft instead of the cold steel in my voice box. I lunge forward. It breaks. Some choose not to take part in this. They say: "I do not feel called to break arrows in my throat."

I wish I had thought of saying that, but I am pleased that my mind is strong enough to shatter wood – now for the coals.

The Fire Keeper has brought the burning embers to the meadow. She has built a path from lengths of wood and filled it with glowing coal. Chanting and clapping and cheering we each dance up and down the scorched channel. I do not feel it. I jump and dance. I stand still. I do not burn. The umber rocks cannot harm me. I am elated.

9

UNSOCIAL SOCIETY

Mist and haar drift between the hills. The sky and the sea have been calm for too many days. His hair has grown, it is blond and curly. He has aqua-eyes. He is tanned and lean, and he has steel toe-capped boots and woollen socks on his feet.

You see him and run to him, and he lifts you high and swings you around. He reaches in his pocket for a lollipop, unwraps it as you gaze at him, hands outstretched. He sets down his backpack for you to examine. It is to each others' eyes that ye speak. Mouths move but you are drawn into each other as though drinking. You pull out a teddy to squeeze and love and bathe in mud. Next, some train tickets from a trip he recently took. He describes the train with his cheeks puffed out and his arms making chugging motions as though old locomotives still operated in the Highlands. He'll find boxes, he says, make a train. You tell him you already have a box-bus but when the cross lady came I took it away.

"A Social Worker," I tell him. I look away. He does not react, which is unusual. But, maybe his Mother told him already. I know now that he told them. It was he who phoned them. I cannot ask because of his temper.

"I can't get the bus down here, but it's full to the gunnels with shopping for ye. There are a few bits here for a picnic but I'm gasping for a coffee. You'll find some whisky in the bags of shopping. There were bargains galore. Any chance you'd fill that flask and meet us down on the shore?"

"I'll be down in a minute. Business must be good if you're spending your earnings on supplies for us."

Displays of generosity reward him with attention. I need him to ask about the social worker. I have to ask him why he left a joint but he's brought a sack full of a Daddy's love for you and will fill my cupboards. I cannot challenge him about the joint. He may have left it for me. I'll not ask him, I won't row with him. I need him too much; thank him instead, kiss him passionlessly.

I fill the flask; put fruit in a tub; a feeding cup of goats' milk; cups; alfalfa; sprouts; almonds – the offerings the posh guest house guests leave behind.

He is dangling your podgy toes in the ripples of the dying waves. The boots are off. The plaid is hitched into his belt. Neat ankles gleam white; have not been exposed to sun or tourists. The dog stands in the shallows and tries to catch your splashings, but the salt water irritates her and she coughs. You squeal and squeal. He is letting out a deep, belly laugh. Everyone grins. The simple normality may break me.

Since the ceremony I have been attempting to acknowledge and honour my emotions, my sadness's, my Dreams. I grieve for the mistakes I have made. The stupid stuff I have done, the lies, the deceit, the games I play – my lack of integrity to either myself or my heart. I yearn to turn back time, face my truth rather than plan a life of deception. In the wooden box my Papa made I have a leather bound book. It was a gift at the Fire Walk. I scribble the stories that have made me sad and balance them with dreams of happy times. I write in the night when the owls call. Each sentence is written as though my Mother were reading it.

All hope is sealed with this picnic into this ice cream tub, to be handed to the man in the plaid. To do with what he will. Your Father will not return, will not greet his progeny with greater emotion than this man. The dark one will never beg for forgiveness from his small daughter. He will never offer sweets and surprises and unconditional love. He is not able. He cannot forgive me. The light plays on the stones and you reach down and try to catch the prisms.

"Do you two want a bit of food at all?"

He is hungry. He wants more than these few bits. I have no more to give him.

"Mary, you're looking well. Have you done something different to your hair? My Ma was saying I should speak with you. I'm hoping there's nothing wrong. She was looking awful pleased with herself, so she was. She wants you for her own wee gang you know."

I tackle it with tact. I manage him because I want to keep him. Or use him. Because you love him and he loves you. I explain easily.

"It is not a life-change for me. I do not want to convert to this as a way of life. I know that to attend the Free Church is a safer thing to do. But I have had such a sheltered life. It's interesting and I am learning. Learning how to let go of all the hurt and frustration, all the different ways to love and express myself."

I play him, lower my lids; look away wistfully. Vulnerability can be strength, she said.

"He hurt me you know, when he rejected his child. I'd better deal with that. I can't let it fester. There's things go on in this world I had no idea of. It's an education, illuminating".

"Like what? What has she involved you in?"

"Well, I did the Fire Walk and the Sweat Lodge, and that was fun. I broke an arrow with the power of my mind. I met some fabulous people. And I saw the goddess ceremony."

"The what?"

"It's like a sex ritual thing."

Oh no. I'm talking about his Mother having sex with another woman, with a dildo, whilst wearing antlers and surrounded by chanting women. I should shut up. I hope there's a stage in the development of an adult where the brain interacts with the voice and stops the conversations that lead to insult and injury.

"Ritual sex? Are you serious?"

Does silence mean yes or no?

"Where was Angel?"

Oh, he is so sweet. He thinks of you first. But how do I hold onto him and still explore my own nature – especially when the man seems to have every good reason in the world to abhor the realms beyond the veils. And in this moment, in this thought, I have understanding of him.

This is the dilemma Gertrude faced. She chose to leave him.

"She was with me but we left before she saw anything too graphic."

"What was she doing?"

"She was calling a goddess."

"Did she have that old grey strap-on?"

"Aye, and antlers."

"Were there many there?"

"About a dozen."

"That strap-on is older than me. She found it in a museum and stole it. Said it was hers in her previous life. She's mad,

I told you. She's off her head. Stay clear."

He is holding back. Words are forming that cannot be spoken. His colour is changing from a healthy tan to the shade of a bruise. He is retreating into some place inside himself. He stares out at you. I can feel the little tremors running through him. He presses his lips down tight together, stares up into the sky.

"The clouds are coming in, looking all thunderish. We might have to be heading off in a minute."

"There was a Social Worker came here one day a few weeks ago, a couple of polis, too. They found one of your joints. I've got to go to town, make a statement and be investigated, and go to some parenting classes."

"This is what I'm talking about. Ye can't be staying here for too much longer. You pair will be destroyed here. There's only one way to get on here on this island. This isn't it. Tomorrow we'll go back to the local Church."

"Monday I'll take you into the town and you can make the statement and see the social services. Then get the benefits sorted out and put in for another council house. Move down south, there's good opportunities down the south end of the island now. With a bit of Gaelic you might get a job. There's a great wee nursery for herself. I should never have brought ye here. I should have known. Me Ma plays on the vulnerable folk. I should have known better. But I didn't think she'd do it again."

That was smooth. Seamless. An alarm jingles in my head. He knew. Maybe his mother told him. That speech was definitely planned.

"Listen, there's something I'd like to do. I like what she does. I like opening up to the world and the universe and the powers of Nature. It is wonderful to listen to the other women and realise that they are just as insecure as me. I want to change. I want to meditate every day; eat healthily; listen to my heart and my intuition. I really want to do another of these workshops, just one, and then I'll leave all this stuff alone. But I would love to see the vision quest on Lewis. Just to see. I think it would help me, you know, be stronger and put the past behind me. You could come, take some tourists. Go on, and say you will. Say you'll mind Angie. Please?"

They are almost identical when they think, a scheming pair that scratch their faces when plotting.

"Aye. The Drum Dance, I've seen it. Five days fasting and dancing and hoping to get so off your face that you slip into the world of spirit and get a vision. Load of pish."

He doesn't think I'll cope. He fiddles with a bristle of hair on his chin. He is almost dismissive. There are large thoughts absorbing his attention. I will not know all of them. As the weather front covers the surface of the sea, so the harmless blue becomes hard in his eye. The brows swing down. I have hurt him. Simply registering my interest in the Other Ways frightens him.

"Mary, you're gorgeous. You're looking better and better every time I see you. You're doing real well since you moved here and I'm glad you got out of that housing scheme, but I'll not ask again, so, here's the deal girl, I'll mind the wee one 'cos I love her with all my heart, but I can't watch you go on this quest. I can't. I've seen it too many times. I don't want to lose you. Don't want to lose Angel. But I'm backing away from you while you do this. Can't watch another kid get messed up in this nonsense. There's the rain cloud coming in. Looks like thunder."

Big drops fall. The dog slinks off. Black tinges the edges of our world. Thunder comes. We have to run back to the caravan. He scoops you up and shelters you in his big arms. A piece of his cloth is wrapped around your head. I watch you go.

He has made hot chocolate. You sit and sip from a cup he holds to your lips. I am drenched because I picked up the picnic things and his pack.

"That was a good wetting you got," he laughs, "look, Mamma's all wet," and you both giggle like crazy girls.

"Did you meet my sister? She came for the Fire Walk?"

"No," I lie to him. "No, I did not meet your sister".

"I'll away to get the stuff from me bus. See if she's still about. I'll bring her down. She hasn't been in contact with Ma for quite a few years. Only I knew where she was. It was herself loaned me the cash for the bus. I suppose it's hers really. I have managed to forget to pay her back, shame that, with all the cash from the Yanks in the bank. She has been living in Devon in some sort of intentional alternative community. I understand from her last text messages that she has found some sense and is ready to quit the world of the lesbian white witches. I'll get her to have a word with you; you'll get on well, the pair of ye."

He would leave me. He would go if I said I wanted to explore the inner workings of myself. If I told him that I need to let go of pain and embrace joy he would run a mile. He's afraid. He is the one who would benefit most from healing. I'm afraid of a life without him.

He returns with only bags of shopping. No sister. He takes out a bottle, opens it, pours two glasses, adds water to mine. He has another speech prepared.

"Opening your mind to all possible universes within this universe is possible. But it is not easy. Great thinkers and scientists have tried. Native Americans selected one from each generation to hand secrets and knowledge to. It is not supposed to be accessed by all. Unhappy women cannot turn to Shamanism because it offers a wee change from housework. It's a gift, a calling. You cannot abuse it. You don't know what you're messing with. The human mind is an astonishing place. It can create every reality. But without the correct structures and boundaries it can all go horribly wrong. Respect what you have girl. Don't go messing about in the realms ye don't understand. I've seen folk believe all sorts and I've seen my Ma encouraging them to believe the crap because then she gets paid for treating them and healing them."

The gentle swagger is gone. The broad back is stooped. Deep trenches have appeared between his eyebrows. There's no bravado. He is not boasting or trying to impress. He cares.

"Mary, you have absolutely no idea what could potentially happen in this life. There is no way you can accurately see the future or what will happen to you or your child. You cannot control any of it. All you can do is be the best you can be in any moment. Read your Bible 'cos there's some fine tips on how to behave on this planet in this lifetime. Study theology if ye like. But please please please don't go listening to my crazy loon of a mother. I mean antlers? Antlers?"

"I want something different. I want something else. I want to see a different way".

"You're talking like a spoilt brat. I want. I want. You have a responsibility to that wee kid. That's all you're going to do for the next few years. That's it. I don't want to fall out with you, really, I don't. But you have to start hearing me. Just look after Angel. Just do that. Quit the carry-on with the maddies."

He is threatening now. He has some plan worked out. I can see it. I can see the utter determination to stop me. I think I am being oppressed or suppressed or something and I do not want to listen or see his point of view.

"A while ago you asked me to put my name on her birth certificate saying I was her Father. Well, I'll do it. I found out who her real Dad is and he seems to have some issues alright and I don't suppose he'll care either way. We could do it Monday when we go for the statement and all that."

Rain like hail bounces on the tin roof. The sky groans. Flashes dance. We drink and we argue all night. You sleep. He tells of the game that must be played. The united family will attend church; show a respectable face to the social services and the police. He lauds the structure of organised religion, says it is the safest way to raise children. He will display a perfect Mom to the judges and the gossips.

We go to Church. I wear my new green skirt. He shakes hands with all the men. They appear to congratulate him, like he has won an award for rounding up sinners and bringing them here. I am the sinner: the only one to have had sex outside of the sanctity of marriage, the only one caught.

"Do you think it was one of these ones that grassed you up?" He stares around the bare room. Other heads wear hats; are bowed low. He is a distraction. I can neither think nor meditate, nor relax. It is his constant question. Different ways are tried but the conversation remains the same, a one-sided investigation into who called the police. He points to a lilac and lace bonnet, revealing the despicable gossipmonger underneath. A sweetheart of an old dear, he paints her as a lonely, interfering hag. The service continues and so does he.

"See yon biddy with the brown check scarf? Well, she used to be the drinking buddy of my Ma's neighbour. You know, that big old crofter that always wants to wed her? Well, that wifie had her own designs on him. Her man died leaving a poor pension, she needs to supplement her income. I bet she'd do anything to upset things on our croft. Aye, it was her maybe. I wouldn't be surprised at all. She'll see you as another rival, knows you'll need a man to support you. And that big fella has plenty money."

By the time we leave I am pale and paranoid. My stomach begins to churn. I try to gather you in my arms as you leave Sunday school, but he steps in front of me, picks you up, sits you on his shoulders. I stand with the women wondering who hates me the most. My skirt is too green, my head is bare. I do not fit in here either. I imagine them blethering about me; about my weird ways.

Back at the caravan he plays shop and trains. You build towers together. I lie on my bed and smoke. I numb my mind. I write that I want to dance as my Mother did. I need to remember her ways. She was strong. She had sense sewn into the material of life. No man squashed her. No bit of life's lesson intimidated her. She kept house and family rolling together in love. She kept her mind intact, her integrity firm. She wrapped me in her arms whispering how best to live my life and I did not listen. I did not heed my own Mother. Come back and tell me again, this time my ears are open.

* * *

Wood smoke from the burner has timbered your hair, and tickles my nose. Your bum is embedded in my belly. You fart, fidget, snore. The smell wafts through the nappy, up from the blanket. We are foetal, we are twins. Surrounded by my arms, so peaceful, so heart-stoking wonderful. I gave birth to my own twin, half my soul.

The robin and her fat daughter wait, twittering for breakfast. The door creaks open and the perfect moment is gone. He is here. Woof scratches too-long nails on the cheap lino. Her tail thumps on the Formica.

Wallace comes and stands at the foot of the bed. He smells like a cathedral. His jaw is shiny. His eyes narrow; reveal too much. In that moment he is vulnerable. I see his Mother clearly dripping out of him, the way she may have been, fifty years ago, all newly-deflowered and girlish. The sight of us has somehow jarred his fragile ego. I feel his confusion. A little voice in my head tells me he seems jealous. To massage his feeling I pinch my nose saying, "it stinks over here". He appears to forget the sadness he may have opaquely felt.

Instead, he holds out a garment, a dress on a pink, satin, padded hanger; a pink and purple satin dress with taffeta and bows – gorgeous, your size.

"E-Bay, sister," he says. He winks to acknowledge his enterprising ways.

You have no shoes, I think, to do that creation justice.

He produces a pair of welly-boots with cherries on them, and a rain jacket to match.

"New from a shop," he says. He makes his eyes sparkle, puts the chiselled chin at a loftier angle.

He comes closer so that I can more accurately examine his offerings. He is wearing tan chinos. They cling to his ass. The neck of his new kilt shirt is open, leather laces unbound. Someone else's jacket makes him appear smart. He looks like a bit of rough in a clothing catalogue. I think he's going to kiss me and I half close my eyes but instead, he goes to put the kettle on. The day begins.

I roll you away. You stretch into a starfish shape. I follow him. He is glowing with cleanliness. He has anointed himself with some aromatherapy oils. I detect the frankincense again, see the sheen glister on his cheek, the side of the clean shorn throat. A hump is brewing between his shoulders from all day at the wheel.

The kettle whistles. He takes it before I can place a bid for a mug full. He pours it into the blue basin, adds some organic, baby, soapy suds. He tuts mercilessly at the still-damp towel; opens the door on the burner to find some warmth. Soot blackens the pad of his hand; he looks for a cloth or a tissue or kitchen roll in order to keep himself clean. I stand and hand him what he needs, refill the kettle for the desired coffee. He smokes a roll up in liquorice paper. The red breasted family lament the lateness of breakfast. You sigh deeply. Murmur into morning. I go to greet you, lie down again, smell you; shower you with kisses. I beep the little nose, jingle your ears. I tell you that when you were born there was a tag attached to your toe. It said that this baby must be tickled at least twice a day. When we come back into the living space, you stretch your arms to him, you sit sweetly in the bowl of froth, you giggle when he washes your hair and of course you stand and twirl when he places the taffeta over your head. I slink off with the grey water; run the corner of a towel into it and under my arms.

You both look gorgeous. His mood seems stable, but there is no way of really knowing. He may blow at any moment. I have not learned yet to do exactly as he wishes. I pray for a day without his tantrums. I pray that I may do exactly as he wants me to do.

We step by the raised beds. The planks I have nailed together to create growing spaces, spinach, late lettuces. One cauliflower like a faded brain lurks amongst some purple cabbages in a bright blue box. Plastic bags on sticks crinkle the air. Marigolds add gold. You helped me paint the boards; we were all day sloshing brushes at the carrot site and giggling and not bothering to wash the paint off our bodies all week. Your hand prints, foot prints adorn the sides of the boxes. We drew pictures of carrots and put them in plastic bags, tied them to sticks so that we would know what grew where, but the damp has seeped into the sandwich bags making the colours run. The place looks like a home for handicapped rainbows.

We walk around the side of the croft. Wallace has new leather boots on. He leads. You are picked up out of the gorse to ride his shoulders. He strides up the hill. The dog joins in a chase with three collie dogs. The old crofter is out on the hill. I wonder how his dandruff is. A young buzzard screams at them. New rabbits run in hope of safety. A hooded crow tears at a corpse until the dogs come. He doesn't raise his midnight gimp mask until the soft, warm belly dribbles from his beak. The snap of a jaw and the beat of wings on the breeze. Long pink tongues lap and then chomp the rest.

He stands and waits for me at the top of the hill. Looking around, he nods to the crofter and the darkness at the edge of the island.

"The wellies and jacket are new. I bought them in a shop in Edinburgh. She'll need them today – sure gonna piss down later."

One of the dogs rubs her mane into the spilled blood.

He runs his eyes over my body. I smile up at him. I see that he is worried; my clothes are not good enough. This image will let him down.

"We'll have to take you to the charity shop."

I grin and look delighted with his very generous suggestion.

There's a quiver on his face. Today is important, for him. He may cry at any moment. My hand finds his and my body asks. The black surge creeps over the land. Large drops fall from the sky. He turns and runs with you to the bus. I arrive wet. There are presents on the dashboard. There are no tourists. The baby seat is behind his seat. You have a clean tea towel wrapped around your neck, eating tiny organic rice cakes as he spoons fromage frais. He passes me his tin. You ignore me. He has cheered up. He has cheered up. It is sole control of you he wants. Maybe he also craves control of me.

There are no gifts for me. There is a large china doll on a stand for you. Soft handmade paper roughly covers a book. You nod off listening to the wheels on the bus with an oat cake in each hand. The dog sits at my feet and stares up with all-knowing eyes. I wish I knew what she knew.

"The appointment's at eleven."

"Play it different," he says.

"Hey, sister, no guns blazing today. Don't go in there with your mad eye stares. Don't go getting out your dagger and stabbing one of them. They know. We all know that you're a strong independent woman. But still, you just gotta pay some rent, get your paperwork and the child benefit sorted out. It's only a game. Think what it is that you normally do in there, and think what the opposite would be and now do the opposite. This is just an exercise in public relations. I do it all the time. Just tell them what they want to hear. Look them in the eye and do what you have to do. Don't tell them anything else. Don't tell them you are searching for yourself or trying to heal your hurt or your past lives. They are right and you are wrong. They can give you money, and you can get it from them. Smile. Cry a little. Be humble and feminine."

He wipes some fluff from my face. I know now how he gets by. He lies, he flirts; he just does what he can to get what he wants. But, does he want me, or you? Or does he just want to punish his Mother?

First stop, the Registry Office. Out the door of the van you swing between us. One, two, three and ups-a-daisy, all the way up the street. The dog sniffs the lamp posts, and appears to be in doggy heaven.

We arrive at the registry office, fill forms, file, smile. When we leave he is legally your Father. Instead of 'Father Unknown' there's calligraphy declaring Wallace MacGurk as responsible.

We hunt through the dross of strangers. We mingle with the minging. You scramble under whirligigs searching for sparkly, strappy sandals. Eventually, a faded Monsoon jacket completes an Asda T-shirt from the bargain bucket, and a pair of wide legged linen pants slightly too short. We find high heeled shoes. I hate them but he loves them. He pretends to photograph me; makes frames with his fingers to encourage me to believe I am model-like. I am under no allusions. My old clothes are bundled. The new ones make me scratch before leaving the shop. The charity shop has fleas. Halfway down the street and I already have a rash.

He buys me a hair brush and some fancy bobbles in the pharmacy. I choose a foundation, blusher, eye shadow and mascara is added. Tomorrow we will paint your doll. In the public toilets he supervises my transformation. I feel like I am in drag.

"We'll show them. Look at us, we look fantastic. Aren't we the finest, most decent looking family anyone ever saw?"

"It's the initial impression that counts. They only care what you look like. You need to get out of wellies and old clothes.

People judge on appearances. Start caring what others think of you. I know all about this game. Stop scratching."

My reflection glares from a shop window – too much blusher on pale skin, the foundation ending abruptly at the jaw line; clothes that neither suit me or feel comfortable. An unbearable itch makes me seem one hundred per cent more nervous than I actually am. I can feel the fleas biting. I look like the guilty party attending court. Inside my head a battle rages between my favourite inner personalities and their sworn enemies.

Frizz is in. She is still wearing the rainbow striped cardigan.

"I am pleased to see you Miss MacKinnon. I am glad you have brought some support. I have an urgent errand to run; I will be back in a few minutes."

We are directed to the waiting area, an ancient jack-in-the-box on a scratched table, some bricks to stack and knock over. This silly, weak woman bites at long- gone nails, breakfasting on my own flesh. He sits. He sits and he grins, and he is Lord and Master, and suddenly I think I hate myself more than I hate him. You bang the bricks. You clap.

"What'll you do now with all the money coming in?" He asks, "It'll be back-dated you know. There'll be a few months of it. At sixty squid a week you'll be looking at a few hundred, maybe half a grand. Will you move or get a telly?"

"I have been wondering about this dance ceremony on Lewis. I would like to go. Apparently you have to make a donation. And I'll have to pay for the ferry, and a babysitter." I cover my mouth with my hand. Suck my sore fingers like a bear after honey.

Immediately he changes. He pushes all the air out of his lungs with a prolonged wheeze. He makes that disappointed countenance that will work with teenagers. His right foot bangs repeatedly against the side of the chair.

"Can you not see?" he hisses, "...can you not see that ye should stick with me? I am all ye need. You do not need to go exploring how your flaming heart works or how to reduce your Karma so that your soul can evolve more freely. Ye'll do just fine for me the way ye are, not heeding the greater good of the flaming planet. Anything you wanna know, I'll teach you."

He doesn't expect a response. Frizz returns. She remembers our van, the ancient knickers drying across the window.

"I had forgotten my cannabis roll-up. It was intended for my Mother, who, as you are aware, has glaucoma, amongst other problems. I wish to apologise and to attempt to explain myself." He explains that we were dating but are no longer together. He is as contrite as a catholic. He sounds English; middle class. She doesn't believe him. I don't believe him. You look at him wondering why he is speaking in a strange accent. He is over burdened with bonhomie.

"Mary had been experiencing some difficulties with her neighbours here in town. I offered her some respite out at my Mother's croft. She is now isolated entirely and has been unable to communicate effectively with the benefits officer for lone parents thus jeopardising her income support claim. Then of course we all know how demanding two year old temper tantrums can be."

The air has been sucked out of the room. You and I stare at him. You howl. I excuse myself and leave. We pace the corridor, you in my arms. I inhale and count. I calm. You are comforted; tension in the air brings out the worst in babies – and their Mothers. When we return they are shaking hands. They have swapped Vista Print business cards. He is still livid with me for mentioning the dance.

"A Vision Quest is a way to face your fears." He hisses in my ear.

"What's your fear, Mary? What'll you do with a vision? What sort of vision do you think you'll get?" He leaves the room. He takes you with him. She waits for me.

"Miss MacKinnon. Mary. May I call you Mary? Good. Mary. There are a few wee things I would like you to do. Now, this is all quite common, so we will try to do what we can. First of all I will make a doctors' appointment for you, just to assess your physical fitness and see how your stress levels are responding to your new environment. I can probably get you seen before the end of the day. So, while you are waiting, Dad has offered to take the wee one to the ball pool. Come and meet a colleague of mine, she has an office down the hall. She is 'Working For Families'. Well, they do exactly what they say on the tin. Dad tells me you have a wee bit of Gaelic? Well, maybe you could learn a bit more and try for some work with the Gaelic college? I'll refer you to agencies who offer advice and befriending. You don't have to be alone. I'll speak to the police regarding the statement. Don't worry. We'll take care of everything now. I'll get the name of whomever it was you spoke with down at the Job Centre just now."

She picks up the telephone, dials a number, mutters something about a young woman in crisis. Emergency intervention. I have an appointment in one hour with a GP locally. Then we march down the hall and knock on a door.

"Come in" says a voice.

Frizz mutters. A little lady listens.

"Well, I'll see what we can do, shall I send her back up to you or should she go straight to the surgery? Has her daughter already gone to the ball pool with the Dad?"

Frizz nods, pleased her information has been assimilated so efficiently. Delighted to succinctly avert catastrophe, she leaves.

"Would you like a cup of tea? Or an apple? We got fresh apples this morning, they really are very good. We have herbal tea. Or maybe you would prefer coffee? I might have a cup of coffee, seeing as you're here. But I haven't got any biscuits."

She boils the kettle. I stand in her way and scratch. The fleas are delighted with me. The eye shadow begins to harden. I rub it. It streaks. The heels of the new shoes have caused cramp in my calves. I can't take them off because I know my feet smell. I slump into a plastic chair.

We drink good coffee. We each eat an apple. She is easy to talk to. I used to sit and drink coffee and eat an apple with my Mother. This seems similar. I chat. All the words come out in no particular order. I tell her everything I can think of. She nods. She has heard it all a million times before. I tell her I try to write it all down in a letter to my Mother. I tell her we have just registered Wallace as your Father and that it was a lie. I tell her I am afraid of him, but afraid of losing him. I even tell her about his twin, how graceful and loving she seemed. I tell her all about Gertrude, about the Shamanism, the Fire Walk, the Meditations, the healing hands, the past life regression. She tells me that we all search for meaning – sometimes we are fortunate enough to find it. I tell her about his temper, the sudden violent mood swings; the control he exerts over us, the accusations. She asks me why I tolerate it and hands me a leaflet about self esteem. She asks if she can come and visit me sometime and I tell her that would be lovely. She gives me a soft tissue for my eyes, tells me to dab, not rub, that the skin under my eyes is delicate. She asks me if she can document our conversation.

I say 'yes'. Then it is time to go to the surgery.

"Thank you," I say "it was lovely to meet you."

The doctor asks me to fill in a form about how I am feeling in relation to last week, whether I will feel this way next week, and if I ever contemplate suicide. It is to measure possible post-natal depression. I simply tick all the yes boxes. The boxes cannot quantify how I feel or what I have done. They have no insight into the situation I now find myself in. There is lie upon lie. The game is too far gone. The layers of my mistakes cannot be justified, examined or treated by filling in a questionnaire. Generic sweeping generalisations cannot, will not, offer any modicum of salvation or salve. I have done some daft things in my time, but this, this is ludicrous. The wrong name is on your birth certificate. You have a pretend Dad. You may never know the truth. Teeth gnaw knuckles. You have a family. You have history of your own, yet I have denied it. There are loving arms with your own blood and genetics waiting for you. But I have alienated them. I have thrown myself in with a set of dysfunctional, damaged humans, and in doing so I am learning that our own circumstances were perfectly adequate. I am my own worst enemy. The doctor prescribes an anti-depressant, tells me to run to the pharmacy before it shuts. I don't bother. I do not believe it is I who needs the medication. It is him; he needs help. He is the one who needs to examine his past, redress the balance with his own family. Let them all go to family therapy, to scream and shout at each other, to pull at their hair and their clothes, and finally be honest about how much they hurt when their father left and their Mother went mad. Leave me alone. Leave me out of the game, out of their equation. I go back to the bus and retrieve my bundle of old clothes. In the public toilets I wash and change.

10

THE BENGAL TIGER

There is one tree. It has lost its leaves. It looks like an old withered man staring out from the edge of the sea.

Wallace is kneeling in the heather. You are beside him, standing into his shoulder and his arm. He points out across the water. He begins a story.

"Long, long, ago there were giants stomping up and down from island to island, huge men and women. They were higher than the hills. They were hairier than the heather. Every twenty years they grew taller because they wanted to reach the stars. The land was flat then. Winds were stronger. Nothing grew. The Hebrides were low, boring places. The skies seemed so much brighter and more interesting that they wanted to get bigger and bigger, to stand one on the shoulders of another until they could pull stars nearer to them. They wanted to live with the star beings."

Up on the shoulders you go with still-podgy hands aiming for stars. The spindly twigs of the old man tree wave. His head lolls into the wind, springs back again. A movement which will be beautiful when the green season comes again, clothes him in the finery he surely deserves.

"The people of the stars did not want to be pulled to Earth by the big giants. Like children, they wanted to be free to float and drift amongst the moonbeams. Like fairies, they wanted to flit and find mischief. They wanted to control the bigger people. They sent bright lights of all colours to hurt the Giants' eyes. The giants got cross. They threw rocks from the seas into the darkness of night. A great battle was fought between the giants and the star people. But, they folkies way on up in the sky, well, they had magic and they brought it to Earth. First of all they put a spell on the big giant men and they made them their slaves. They had to lift the sides off cliffs, then dig holes to put them in. The giants had to gather the biggest, jaggiest lumps of stone, bigger than you and I, but the same size as the ancient people. They wanted the edges of the rocks to point upwards. So the stones were all put in a line, and another line and another line until they had made a pattern. A circle was made in the middle. It was a very particular sort of shape for the spaceship to land on, so that more star folk could come.

"That's what we have behind us, the Callanish Stones are really a kind of airport runway. It was built by the old people of this place. When it was finished, the star folk put a terrible spell on all the giant women. The lights danced across the skies making them all go to sleep. One by one they lay down just where they'd been standing, and fell asleep. Greens and pinks swooshed across the night sky. The giants had never seen such pretty dancing colours. The big giant men were imprisoned forever inside the stones. And they're still asleep today.

"See now, follow my finger out over the loch; there's one of them over there. There she is, lying down, from that mountain and on to the shore. That summit is her forehead. There's her nose and her chin. Big boobs, a fine figure. No one knows when she'll wake again. D'ya see, if you look over there?"

"No," You say – the automatic two year old's response.

"See the hill with the gentle slope, well, that's a pillow for her head".

"Is this Cailleach na Mointeach?" I say.

"If you just said Sleeping Beauty then aye, that's right. See her stretching all the way down there? Can you see her, wee Angel? See the humps? Well they're her boobies and her belly".

We are in a wild, one-tree place – The Isle of Lewis. A puddle of water slips around the side of the bit of land. It looks harmless now. But all Scottish sea lochs are adept deceivers.

"This old thing is a menhir: 'men' from the Breton for stone, and 'hir' for long. Big old long stones. See babe, this one is way, way bigger than me. It nearly touches the sky. Remember now, don't go staring at pretty lights in the sky. If you see Aurora, be kind to her but don't let her notice you – she might turn you into stone too!"

Lewissian gneiss is like wood. The way the stone ripples is like the bark on a tree, rough and full of character. The Earth Mother relaxes along the skyline. For her head she has a field of purple heather. Her torso seems to be an old derelict croft, left fallow. There is no doubt now; the female form represented so immaculately by the land. It is not known how long she has slept. He tells us that the tallest stone was erected 3000 years BC. I run my hand along the surface, note the cup marks, the fringed edges, the shapes. Maybe there is a mysterious phrase to be spoken thrice aloud to release the slumbering lumps? Perhaps words of love from his lady opposite. We stand on a very small tor surrounded by these great obelisks, and an ocean of bog. This is Loch Roag, Gaelic for cold place. Callanais is older than Stonehenge by over five hundred years. The bare tree sways.

He has sulked for weeks. He has grumbled endlessly about this trip. I had to pay him. I had to give him my back-dated child tax credit to take me here and to look after you while I embarked on this quest, search for the meaning of this life we find ourselves in.

"Most Mothers on these islands dream of filling their freezers for the winter. Not you, Mary. Some women book weekends away in health spas or sit and relax with pals or their families. I had thought, Mary, with you being a beautician an all that you'd like to do something like that. I never thought it'd be this crap that'd float your boat." He said.

"Did you not fancy sipping pureed cucumber smoothies whilst a foreign masseuse rubbed oils into your aching shoulders? Disappear for a week to sunny Spain? Or invite Granny to stay?"

It is the beat of buffalo hide that calls me, the tapping of fingers and palms on the sides of a drum, to dance, faster and faster. To shake with the rattlesnake rattle; to go without food and water for five days; to sleep beneath the mysteries of heaven and earth; to swing these hips in ancient prayer, all day and all night on the bare, Lewis land, in time with the drum. Stare at the earth and the sky and beg for help. The Cailleach will inspire me. She will be my focus, my totem. Like the Virgin Mary for my Catholic ancestors, I will ask for the skills of an Earth Mother.

"Here comes Sue."

Sue is tall. Her hair is grey. Her skin is smooth. She has lovely soft eyes.

"Did I say never?" He greets her with his most manly stance.

"It was ten year ago when I said never. You said then never say never now here I am bringing you a Dancer."

"We cannot escape our chosen path, Walter."

Walter? Gertrude called him that a long time ago. I dismissed it then; took no notice. I am more awake now.

He looks at me with a snide smile, with eyes that have been found to be lying. The flirt begins.

"Sue, you know right well that I changed the name a long time ago now. Call me Wallace, 'tis more in keeping with the image of the Gael."

He touches her arm.

"Walter, I have known you all your life. The image of the Gael is the disguise you wear, not one you were given at birth. It does not feel real to me. I remember your vow not to return to the ceremony, your decision to rebel against your Mother's lifetime of hard work. Children do this sort of thing. We all find our true path. I knew you would return to us." She takes his hand.

"Well, I'm no returned. I'm bringing this woman here. I'm bringing her because she's stubborn and will not listen to reason. She's determined to dance her heart out. This is Mary. Mary, meet Sue, your Chief. This here is wee Angel." He smiles at you.

"…Pleased to meet you Mary. This man was once my Alpha Dog. My most trusted Helper. I had great hopes and dreams for him, but he has turned away from the ways of the Shaman; his gifts go unused. He has not told you, I suppose. You did not know he has the second sight? I shall say no more. This is not my story to tell. We will acquaint ourselves later at Ceremony. Your Mother is not here yet. At least, I have not seen her.

"She used to bring you to these events when you were a small boy, before all the trouble between her and her family, when you all lived in Holland. Your Mother used to travel long miles with two children so that you would know a different way. Some of your old pals are here. The other children from that time are also grown. Your sister is here too. Winnie is a Moon Mother this year, and now you bring the next generation. This is wonderful – how the circle has no end. Are you camping on-site?" She returns his limb. He takes your hand in his, steps to one side, separates himself from us.

"No. I have a bus, I made beds in it. I'm going up to Stornoway to see some of me pals. Buy a bucket and spade. Take the wee one to the sandy beaches. I don't know that me Ma is coming over. Think she's just got herself married or something."

He is lying. His voice is too measured to be true. The lilt is away. I can see secrets now. His high wall rises. He defends the castle that is his heart.

"Yes," I say. "She has to mind the goats and my dog. She sends her apologies. She was recently in a ceremony that made her more tired than she had thought possible."

I think of the antlers and the ancient artefact that is a dildo, hoping my image is not transmitted into the psychic airwaves here, hope not to betray her unintentionally.

"That is a pity. This family will be reunited here before I die. There has been so much sadness and separation. Gertrude has always been an inspiration for me. I hope she recovers her strength quickly, and I hope you return for the Feast and Celebration. I will look for you. I will find a special present for your little girl. Mary, if you would like to say your goodbyes then you can come with me. There is much work to be done."

She stands and waits with her head slightly bowed as we nervously embrace. You have been promised a pink spade and an ice cream with a chocolate stick. You do not care that your Mother will be gone for a week. You have pretty shells to find.

I do not cry. I kiss you. I kiss him; let my tongue out onto his lips so that I can taste the salt air. He looks like I have violated him. I stand as you depart. I forget to send angels to watch over you. The naked tree shakes both arms at no one in particular. A buzzard screeches, dives feet first into the expanse of bracken.

Chief Sue and I walk around the site. She wears no feathers in her hair but carries herself with serenity. Her clothes are plain, unlike the many coloured outfits that others wear. Most have feathers, either on heads or dangling around necks. Eagle feathers mainly. Sue shows me the windmill, it is to power the kitchen, a vast tented space. Diverse groups meet here to share a meal. Debates lull as Sue approaches. A Japanese Reiki Master offers her some specially imported tobacco as a blessing. Pots bubble. Coffee stings the air. A stack of dishes waits beside a bucket and a hose for a volunteer. A group of Native American Indian women sit with shaven-headed Buddhists weaving willow and reed fencing for the enclosure of The Great Circle. Tokens have been brought from their home countries, they are laid out on a multi-coloured blanket for the many free-range children to admire.

The Chief tells of the history of Lewis to the foreigners. Her audience sit. Children are shushed.

"I think the Lewissians were referred to in the ancient writings of the Greek Dioddorus. He described an island to the far north of Greece where the Hyperboreans had built a temple to the god Apollo. A stone temple was described. The similarities are endless. He said that the god danced on the earth once every nineteen years, playing his harp. The island was described as flat with the moon appearing to be very low to the ground. We have calculated that this will occur in five nights' time. We have come from all over this planet to witness this, so that we may tell others, that the events here are as well known as many other, more famous structures. You already know that a large wind farm is scheduled to be built on this blessed spot. It is one of the reasons we have all been called here this week.

"The Pleiades will rise over one line of stones. We petition the people of the stars for aid. We offer this sacred dance. We offer the energies of Light and Love to the Spirits that they may bless us. We ask, through our efforts, that Divine Will be done. This is the ancient land of the ancestors. Friend Eagle has his home here. We will raise the profile; let the local politician see the unique history on his doorstep. This is the hunting ground of Eagle. It is our destiny to preserve it. This is your Spiritual Home; for five days and nights let us sing and dance and pray to the Grand Fathers and the Winds of the Four Directions to save it from the bulldozers and man's greed."

The women begin a meditation; touching a singing bowl, throwing tobacco.

"This is one of our Dancers." I am introduced to this new world. I am filled with fear. I wonder what the rituals are here. I hope there's no sex involved. I hope there's no human sacrifice.

"Your name in this Sacred Space will be Crow Mother. You will learn to love brother Crow, fly like him into the sky with friend Eagle."

How can she know that I hate these hooded crows?

"We will sweat out our toxins in the Lodge later. You will eat nothing, drink nothing. For the dreams to come you must be empty. You will call to Spirit to come and grant you a vision that will help your growth. You will call to the winds of the four directions to come to you. You will call to Mother Moon and Father Sun to shine favour on you. Your Grandparents and ancestors must be petitioned that the old ways be shown to you for honouring. All these people are here to help you. They will hold you in their hearts as you drift into the Other Realms. Their voices in song will transport you through the Vision World."

Across the tent stands a woman. I know her, the shape of her jaw; the way her breast swells, the way she carries herself. I am drawn to her. Her eyes are green; piercing me. There is recognition between us, a connection. Her face is too familiar. I have seen her under a different canvas. The last time I saw her she plucked a lyre. This is the one from the sex ceremony. She knows that I have seen her before, she knows Wallace brought me – Walter, her brother, Walter. This must be Winnie staring at me, with questions clouding her vision. She comes forward with her hand-woven hemp and willow fence. Her heart is too big and must slip out of her eyes.

"Take these to the dance site. We don't want our dancers to be cold."

The smile catches me. I nod, have to look away. The statue in the music room has her face, her countenance. She embodies all her brother cannot.

"Or our Helpers to freeze solid," says an old woman.

"Yes," I say.

At the top of the avenue is a circle with a burial chamber in the centre. There is much discussion here on the significance of this stone circle. It is the camp for the drummers. They say the acoustics are perfect, a miniature amphitheatre. A sacred oak from Sleat has agreed to come. It stands in this inner circle. A buffalo skull has been attached to the top. It looks down the avenue and to the north. The dancers face this. Feathers from eagles and osprey, owl, hawk float from this one tree.

"We will bring Light into the world," says a man.

"By dancing here we will be filled with the Light of Spirit. You must not look at the Helpers, they will not be anointed; they must not see eyes that are in another realm. If you come out of the circle you must wrap yourself in a blanket, keep your head down. Do not speak of your visions; keep the energies sacred, like heavy secrets. Even for Morning Prayer, you must not look into the face of another. This is my sixth dance. After seven my karma will be lighter. Eat now. Drink. You will not have another chance. Sister Dancer, Crow Mother, I give you my love and support and thank you for this great Dance."

Chief Sue lights the fire and then some Sage sticks. We are all anointed. Moon Mothers chant as they corral us together with smoke. They cleanse and purify. The drummers begin a slow tap-tap-tap with tips of fingers on the rim of the leather. The light airy song rises. Only vowel sounds. Two notes. Tobacco is offered in blessings. The dancers are handed chicken bones, symbolising that we are to be as hollow as these bones; we must whistle through them, calling to Spirit to come and grant our vision.

Then there is a large sweat lodge. Spirit is petitioned for many causes. The hurts of the land and the ailments of the people are primary concerns. Conversations regarding the wind farm continue. Elders and officials have created paperwork piles so that this ritual may be carried out on this date. The significance is lost on me. The heat is too great. I do not understand the lines of degrees to the star called Capella. Sweat streams down. I know nothing of the star system called The Pleiades. Many bodies, many hot stones, older, more experienced, hardier beings linger in the steam. I do know that the full moon of September is in five nights' time. I also feel that my life is about to change. I am here to meet my fate.

After the sweat lodge the dancers are given melon. This is to be the last thing we eat or drink for five days and nights. We go to our places. We change into skirts. Then everyone gathers round to sit cross-legged on the ground to watch Mother Moon rise from this sparse place into the fabulous, glittering, canvas above. Sue speaks of the earth as one community and of the stars as an evolved race.

"Dancers go to your places." She calls.

A line of feathers on a rope separates us from the drummers in The Great Circle. We dance up and down always facing the tree, the buffalo skull. We focus on the one feather we chose. We look neither left nor right nor behind. There are four arms of the cross of stones. In each arm there are eight dancers, seven men and one woman. North, south, east and west we dance when bid, rest when told. The drumming on the wind beats its way into our hearts and within a very short time our bodies throb with one rhythm. Every out-breath is a whistle. Hunger comes. Thirst comes. Night falls. I lie on my bedroll. Winnie brings a hot stone to place at my feet, a warm flannel to wipe the dirt from my body, a blanket to keep me warm. I drift to slumber with the stars I adore sparkling above me.

At dawn, the drum beats. The other Dancers rise, pulling blankets about them. Every person is here on the hill to greet Father Sun. We stand together singing the ancient prayers of the Native American Indians.

'Way-oh, way-oh, way-oh, way' is the sound I hear. Bellies echo. Throats rumble. Low and high, deep and ringing, the sounds carry across the moor and the bog to the houses where children wake for bus journeys to Stornoway and school. There will be news in the local houses this week.

All day we march and sway, banging, beating, thumping drums. Every fibre moving, tapping, a pattern shuffled into the moss, a pulse inside and out. Mind is lost, ego gone, only the body remains.

The next day hail comes from dark clouds. We are pelted, yet we continue. My boots become mud-sodden, so I go barefoot. The men strip. Braves with leather whips flay their backs; jump at the centre stone, catching flesh on gneiss. They leap at the totem, bounce off it; one higher than the other. Warriors now, they whoop and shout for war. I search still the Old Woman of the Moors for the answers to Motherhood, over and over and over again. I plead for the strength to raise my daughter, to be released from the learned ways, to honour history by allowing it free passage away over the bleak hills, out of our lives.

Kaku comes out of a great obelisk. His face is so like the pattern the winds have made that I think he has been there all the time. He is larger than when I first met him; that day we went out walking from the Drumlie Dub. He has been part of this rock, the faded ferns gone. Songu reveals herself, her lichen hair sewn onto her stony body.

"You are now on your journey," he tells me. He hands me a flower.

"This small beauty grows after the Great Cold. After pain comes love." It is a snowdrop. It is a vision of a snowdrop.

The sun dries the Stones. Stretching to cut each horizon, they glimmer silver-grey. They seem more slender, taller. I feel smaller. I have to pee. In the toilet tent the window has condensation trickling down it. My tongue is so caked that I lick the window, then, I bend to blades of grass and beg them not to tell as I suck the dew into my desiccated mouth.

On the third day it is bright. Spiders have woven filigree nets all about the machair. I sneak to the toilet after Morning Prayer. I gather the dewy webs and eat them. The thirst remains; guilt is added to it. I cannot blow the whistle because it dries my mouth and uses too much energy. The men still cry, still throw themselves at the Great Stone or the totem. Our hearts beat to the one drum.

You return to me on the fourth day. You swim into my ear. The essence of you coats my brain in jelly, a hot membrane which drips down into my chest. I melt into the love of you. You hold my hand, my heart, as I skip forward and back, forward and back, north to south. The sun is bright in a clear sky. Shapes move in and out of the Stones. The tree-man bows to the lady of the hill; they rise as one to join us in a dance beyond the veils. I sway with them. Then, without warning, you are gone. A large Bengal tiger sits on the top of the totem. She gnaws the buffalo skull. I see her teeth. Her golden expanse leaps at me. I faint. I am carried to my place. Winnie fans me with eagle feathers, covers me with sheepskin; tends a fire with sweet smelling sticks.

The Tiger is huge, each hair moves. She is made of yellow gold. Her eyes are green and real and keen and true. She breathes warm air on to my face. I go with her. Together we hunt on arid plains, fight to feed our cubs. Her voice is deep.

"Go to your child," she says. "Wake now. Go and protect your child. She needs you. She is in danger."

I can only stare, transfixed by her brilliant colours. There is no energy in my body with which to respond.

"Go to your Child," she roars, ruffling my hair with the wind from her mouth.

I sleep. Wallace's twin tends me. Many images come, shadows of memories surface and fall away. The faces my parents wore when young are wrapped up in their hopes, the person they wanted me to be. Their parents in turn display their ways, disappointments, flaws. The time line of great-grand parents reaches back hundreds of years. I see life on these islands has not changed beyond modernisation, legends rooted in someone's dreams. Tales of tears mark this tor, that hillock, now and forever. Love binds us to evolution.

The Bengal Tiger stalks me, batting the velvet paw against my back. She tells me she is my teacher. I must learn quickly, there is no time. It is her I must emulate, not the still hills. Take control. There will be trouble always, someone or something desperate to take you, to destroy you. She says much. She reveals hidden threats, dangers, the obstacles that make a life rich in experience, the troubles that shape. Survival of the fittest – I find myself inside her skin, sitting on top of the totem, gnawing at the buffalo skull. I leer at the Braves. I snarl at the drummers. I slay wildebeest; tear flesh to sustain my litter.

Chief Sue sprinkles powders on the fire. Musty potions poison me. The day goes by and the night also. The Bengal tiger waits beside me.

I wake to witness the full moon rise from between the breasts of the Sleeping Woman. Women sing. Drums beat. Bells chime. Rainmakers rattle. Mother Moon, they call. Winnie stands on the tor with her lyre. I hear a flute. Mother Moon creeps along the shoreline. She is triumphant. Then all is black. Silent. Hours pass. Bright stars appear inside the east wing of the cross. Light returns. Mother Moon joins them.

On the tor, Winnie is silhouetted by the brilliance. Her image is thrown into the Stone Circle, with the moon at her heels and the Pleiades about her head. She appears to dance on land and on the moon whilst playing her lyre. We watch without breath. She is tall. She has become silvery blue. All night the moon, the stars, dance around Winnie in the centre of the stone circle. The Stones glow. Light bounces off their flat, grey bodies.

This light must be visible from space, but no cloud shaped carriage descends. The Borealis does not beckon, green beings go unnoticed. No body from a far off galaxy leans into the miles of stone and bog where Earthlings wait, still chanting the same two vowels from centuries passed – way-oh, way-oh, way-oh, way.

* * *

Dawn on the sixth day, I must go. The Bengal Tiger and I slouch off. I find my holdall beside a gate. When I reach in to find a fleece I find a note from Wallace.

'Due to your altered mental state I have taken my daughter to safety. The social worker is aware and approves. W.'

The Tiger is no longer beside me. She lives and breathes within me. I march down the single track road. I do not go north to Stornoway, but south to Tarbert. My thumb finds a truck delivering frozen pies. Shoeless, starving, clueless I race back to the caravan. The ferry is delayed. The Minch is choppy. The truck driver eyes me, regularly asking if I am quite all right. I can but growl in his direction. I have almost made up my mind to swim the Minch when the CalMac ferry chugs her merry way into port. I have no ticket, no money with which to purchase one, yet no one questions me. I glare. I glower. I pace and fume. They let me on. Someone offers me a drink. I think to rip the eyes from his head. The truck driver cannot take me where I need to be, he has pies to deliver. I flirt a little with him, ask him to buy me a drink in the pub on the pier.

"Whisky," I tell him, when prompted.

The smell of the peat coming off of it causes a gag in the back of my throat. I stare out the window as the waves lick a roll of tangerine weed. He goes for a piss. I go out and steal his pie van and drive like the devil possessed (or an enraged Bengal Tiger) to the back of beyond where time stands forever trapped. I do not crash.

There is no one in the caravan. I sit on our bed, staring at the floor. Something is misaligned. There has been a disturbance in the under bed debris. I open the box my Papa made. Your birth certificate is gone.

11

EATING THE SPIDER WEB

"Angel?" I call.

A bird twitters. The note repeats your absence.

Come now Knight, or never. Charge me with excessive dreaming. Take me. Bind me, stop up my mouth with the leaves fallen on the forest floor. Drag the dirty ropes the fishers forgot into the wood. Secure me to my tree and leave me. I have failed the one I love. I am worthless. Let some dirty crofter find me. Let him take his clarty cock from his manly breeks; the thing only favoured sheep see. Give me more pain. Destroy the core of this woman. Leave me bloodied and quite dead. I have lost my girl. You are gone.

In the caravan, the pictures you drew cover every wall. Crayons, pen-tops, odd socks litter the floor, the chairs, the table. Books with hidden ducks are scattered. A naked doll in a plastic pram waits by our bed. Your belly-laugh hangs in the air, rings my ears and stings my senses. A hand, full of mischief, drew underneath the table. Your image grins from many frames, sparkling little sprite, with eyes that glow with love for Mam.

"Angie?" I cry to the whipping wind.

'Due to your altered....'

God and Angels in Heaven help me. Send me someone to fight for me. I am incapable. Where is the handsome prince we learned about at school? There was no fairy story ever ended so. Mister Charming, saviour of single mothers, does not steal children. Wicked witches, fairies gone bad; they take princesses as slaves. Not the hero.

The Tiger told me. I did not listen. The Tiger said Go! Hot breath on my face, the smell of unwashed teeth: I remember. The wind from her mouth warmed my hair. Had I heeded her, you may yet be here. I stared into sharp pools of hazel-green. True, deep and linked to the One Heart. Stupid woman did not listen. Slept an afternoon. I slumbered the night away with my head in the heavens, my mind a-gog.

'Due to your altered mental state...'

Your constant chatter has ceased. Many times, many times I said 'do you ever stop talking? Do you pause for air?' Now come and yak in my face. Blether 'til my brain falls out. It is silent. There is only the sound of my own negligence.

'I have taken my daughter to safety.'

Redeem my misdemeanours. Take this transgression. I am flawed, deep, deep within. Life and genetics have made me ineffectual. Mother Earth, I lie in your musty places and weep for the frailty of my sex. I thought the man would help me. He strode through Drumlie Dub as my saviour. I seduced him so that he might protect us.

Baby mine, adorable, beautiful bundle of mischief and menace, this job is too grim. I am only one woman, one woman, and one babe, and one dog. Eccentricity flows like bog-water in my blood.

'The Social Worker is aware and approves.'

Oh dear darling tree of life, I wrap my arms about your trunk and beg for mercy. Let me be a tree, my roots anchored solidly in soil, hard and unyielding, bowing to nothing but the great ocean gales. Brown, smooth, dark, craggy, tremendous temple; my forehead lowers. I scratch my face into the crevices. Sex and trees. Trees and sex. Strength. Protection. I will remain here. I will sleep in the soft, downy green; feed on berries; forage for mushrooms.

"Angel?" I scream into the night. Keening, calling like a buzzard longing for a mate. Let me shed this skin.

The Bengal Tiger bats me with a paw, hard.

"No one can save her." She says, "No one but YOU."

The clothes I wore dancing lie in the moss. There is mud on my ankles. I am braless. There is no food in this body. I lie down in the burn with my mouth open. Liquid cleans my mouth. I try to drown but cannot; there is too little water.

I must find you. I must know that you are safe. I must have you back, here with me, with the one that loves you more, and never let you go again.

I walk up the hill. I cry from the door.

"Your son has taken my child. It's all your fault. He is messed up in the head 'cos you abandoned him as a child. You didn't love him enough. Now he's getting revenge by kidnapping Angel. She's gone. He left a note."

The women come. They stare. Elsie is the first to speak.

"Where are your clothes?" She takes the old fluffy cardie off her back to wrap around me.

"What has happened?" Gertrude asks.

"I found out his name is Walter, not Wallace. He lied. He just wanted Angie all the time. He took her."

They look at each other with real fear popping out of their eyes.

"Not again." Elsie says.

Gertrude shakes her head to quiet her.

"We take one step at a time. Child, what have you eaten?"

I explain that I had to leave the Dance early; have not eaten for five days and nights.

"Stupid child," says Gertrude, "you must feast at Ceremony. You discuss vision with Chief and Elders. They make sure you safe. Not run away. It is important to speak with the Wise Ones with the honesty and the open heart, tell all what you have seen."

My feet are dirty. She wipes them with a cloth, lifts first the left and then the right to dress me in her old leggings. Crocs are placed on my feet. I am led through the house and sit on a small stool. Elsie lights candles. A container is taken from the fridge, its contents emptied in a pan on the stove. Oatcakes are passed over to me.

"And no food or drink…ay ay ay…I tell you before that I am doctor, well now you must eat what exactly I give you. In your head there will be much confusion. There will be paranoia's, delusions even. Later we will listen to this story of my son."

Elsie runs me a bath. Then she places a towel on the range to warm. I sip thin porridge. She clucks and tuts. Gertrude calls Chief Sue on the telephone, I hear her ask if he has been seen.

"You have not seen her child? No, it is not his child. Is my daughter there?"

She leaves the room so that she can speak in peace. She comes back with a shake in her hand.

"Dancers do not know what they have seen. Elders interpret the visions; guide Dancers on their Path. More oats now. Some tea. Lie down."

Woof comes to sniff me. She lies beside me with the whites

of her eyes flickering accusations.

"Your girl will be safe Mary," Elsie says.

"It is a lesson for you," says Gertrude, "this is the beginning of the new you. This is the catalyst that will alter you and the way you think forever. It is how the soul grows, you know; through adversity. We all need a struggle to discover what it is we really wanted in the first place. If you write every day the things you think and feel and then after one month you can examine the inner self; decide what to change, what to keep. It will help. One year will pass, you will be like new – the old ways of childish behaviour will be gone. It will be good."

"You will find my Angel before then, won't you?"

"We do not know Angel is missing. We have a sick woman here and we do not yet know what is truth. We can only talk about this when you have food in the body, when you become rehydrated. Just now you are soaring high up on another plane. When you return to your body we will ask questions. Your Chief is asking your fellow Dancers what they may have seen. It is time for you to learn patience. It is time for you to allow another person to look after you. We have been doing this for many years. Do not question us."

Fierce eyes defend their right to old age eccentricities. Younger eyes leak. I dip a dry oatcake in hummus, make pulp of it in my mouth, force it down my gullet.

I suffer the hardest meal. I allow the inquisition. All that I know is told and relayed to Chief Sue; digested by the Dancers and Moon Mothers, bounced off of standing stones and across the Minch, I wait for news.

Then some confirmation comes. He came back on the third day; drove the bus to the site, left a note in my bag and headed south at the crossroads. He took the ferry from Tarbert to Uig.

He was seen at the Cooperative in Portree. You were with him, dripping an enormous ice cream on the clean floor. In Broadford service station he bought you chewing gum and the woman at the counter reprimanded him. You needed a pee at Cluanie Inn. From there the trail is cold.

We do not telephone either the police or the social worker. We wait for the Universal Timing and the Rightness of All Things.

In Elsie's fluffy cardigan I run out to greet the rain. I have judged them and condemned them, sniggered behind their backs. I thought them odd, quite unreal. I thought myself a rebel; flirting with the folk my Daddy warned me about. I praised myself as better than them; juggling child, man and meditation. We wanted to see the stuff that we were made of. We wanted to examine the workings of our hearts. Malcontent misfits peering beyond the boundaries we were given; straying from hormonal bonds. In searching for Utopia, Nirvana melted away and was gone.

I trip over my dog, land in a puddle. There is little left to do but howl. I howl at the moon. The women pick me up, bring me back to the music room; force more watery porridge into me. Camomile tea, rescue remedy, incense from Tibet. I pass out.

* * *

You are gone. You are gone. You are gone. You are disappeared from our bed. It is all my fault. I should never have left you, should never have taken my eyes from you for even a second. I was given charge of you, my beautiful baby. Where are you? Where has he taken you?

The sweet, sweet smell of you lingers. I search down the bed for remnants of my love, my life, my world. Here is a discarded sock, some stray hairs. Here is the head of a doll. I pick the stray hairs, sniff and sniff at them but they have no scent. With frantic pincer movements I pick and gather at them. I examine the colour, the length, extend one to see it bounce back into a curl. I stuff them into the plastic head. I stand by the bed.

Many times I wished for a perfect moment of peace. I wanted just one day of still and utter calm. I wished this too. I wished and wanted it and now it is here. It is all my fault.

This was no way to raise a child, out here in the wilds with just a dog. I should have found family, moved to Mother's relations or Daddy's kin. I should have set a support network in place. Children need families, need cousins and aunts to read and tickle. Children need to chase each other and dare each other to steal sweeties. All you had was this one woman with too much love to give.

The wind rises outside. There's a noise in my head, a heavy weight on my chest. I wanted a baby. The tick tock clock of available years beat through my body. I fucked the first bloke that showed any interest: the selfish gene, this selfish woman. I wanted a baby. I had no consideration of the consequences.

Your Granny would have helped. My Mother, with her soft lilt and her sparkly eyes would have cared for us, given half a chance. But instead I went mad on meditation and fresh air. I failed to love and protect you. I failed the only one I love. And now you are gone.

I pace the short length of the caravan. Up and down, to and fro. The curtains are filthy. There is mould on the windows, thick and green; it is eating at the walls now. Dog hairs line the floor, gather in clumps in corners. Dust from the burner has settled on every surface. The floor is soggy in places.

Here is a page of your scribbling. Maybe it is a note for help. He may have taken you back here while I was still in the land of shamanic vision quests. As I was contacting my inner demons, dancing out my human desires, searching for my own truth, you may have been here. You may have left me this note, this clue. I scan the paper, it may be a map, a letter. I search for words or symbols to decipher, childish hieroglyphics; imaginative meanderings; crayon on paper; red and green and brown lines, swirls and strokes but no sense.

Fold, unfold. Turn it over. There is nothing left of my mind with which to concentrate. I cannot think. I cannot breathe. I pace up and down this grimy hovel with a muddy sock, a doll's head full of your hair, and your last note.

Dear God, dear Mother Earth, dear Universe, Saint Jude of hopeless cases, ancestors, angels and all those who work with and for the Light please come to me now. Help me. Give me a sign that my daughter is safe.

There is a gentle knock on the door. I scream.

In comes Winnie with her hair whipped up. Her face is red and flushed. Her lips stung bright berry red, swollen. But her eyes, her eyes, they dance, they gleam, they bring light from her soul right into my room. She stands with the door open, the wind coming in with her. The dog sees an opportunity, rises from the doldrums, bolts out into the day. Winnie tugs at the bulk of her neon council work jacket, a find no doubt. She peels layers of scarves, swathes of wool, makes a heap of fabrics on the floor. She looks like willow now. Her hands flutter and chatter at me. They dismiss unseen cobwebs, swat the air, swish around me, landing on my head, my shoulders.

Oh! the gentle strength in them. They grasp me.

"I ran down here. I had a sudden urge to see you. Don't call the Police. Don't contact anyone. Please. Not yet. I think I can find them."

"Too late, too late," I want to say, but I don't.

"He can't leave Britain. His passport is in the house. It's expired. It will take time for him to put her on his passport. Why did you name him on her birth certificate? Do you mind if I ask? Talk to me, is it a problem for you to talk to me?"

"Yes, it's a problem for me. I don't know what to say to you. Your brother stole my child. He has my daughter."

She is steadfast, peers at me, treats me to the full glare she inherited from her Mother.

"My Brother, yes. Yes, my brother has done something he shouldn't. Not me. I have not done anything to you. I am not to blame. Do not project your anger on to me. It is misplaced. I will not take responsibility for him. But I will try to help you. I am here to help. Let's talk about it, make some sense of how he feels; understand what happened. Like, what were you doing with my brother? How did you meet him?"

There is a big silence here between us while outside the dog barks.

"How did you meet him?" She repeats.

My fear of confrontation rises in me. This is the point where I would normally run away and hide. I could run. I could. But the hurting heart anchors me. The hope of having you returned makes me stay, keeps me focused. I will walk in truth. I will talk the truth.

"He wandered past my house in the rain one day. I was bored and I was lonely. I saw the adventure in him and I invited him in. We smoked a spliff and I fucked him while Angie was asleep. Then I asked him to leave."

My voice stays strong. Inside I may be having a heart attack.

There are the bones of it, the beginning of the story laid bare. The meat of it is stuck in my craw. I must spit it out.

"You didn't date. You didn't get to know each other. You didn't fall in love. You made no promises of love. There was no discussion. You used him."

Shoulders back, hips thrust forward, thumbs slung in the pockets of her jeans. No flicker over her face, just maybe mirth curled on her lip. She seems happy. She is assertive and I am jealous. She is content with this open conversation. I have mists. I have walls that surround me. My defences are supposed to protect me. They don't. They keep me from you. The brick and mortar moat separates me from you. My meekness must go. Here in this moment, but I feel too insecure to be just me. But she is galling, goading, standing there gently questioning.

"Why did you move out here? Why did you put his name on Angel's birth cert?"

The low voice. The lack of malice. The lack of judgement.

I have swum in fogs for far too long. Smokescreens of my own creation keep me distant from reality. I say and I do anything I please. There is no one to answer to. By refusing personal integrity I can remain aloof. I don't have to get involved. I don't have to be honest. It's easy. But now, this one wee woman demands I explain myself to her.

I stand. There in front of her. I mimic her stance.

"It's the age-old story, Winnie, I just needed some sort of security."

These words are a beginning. The deep well of emotion growls, I think I sound glib, blasé. It is only a little truth. My palms are sweating.

She takes her hands, those little works of art and she taps them on my shoulders.

"Good," she says. Ever more gentle, ever softer, as though she has been and seen much worse than I. I quiver where she touches me. The silence grows huge. The air around us is bruised; sore with the things we cannot say.

I could tell her the sex was awful, that I couldn't orgasm with him. That he knew.

"Come on Mary, where is your coat. You need to get out. The dog is still shouting for you."

Winnie picks up her neon jacket. She lines herself with the returned garments. Again, she looks like a Highland Council road worker, but a beautiful one.

I don't want to go out. I want to stay here and wait for you. Maybe any moment you may just come back, may run down the track with open arms and wide grin. If I just stay here and concentrate really hard, you will hear me, somewhere in your heart and demand to be taken home.

I remember the day I fucked him while you slept. I feel sick. I feel anger. I am worthless, stupid; irresponsible.

"Mary, your coat?"

I don't want to go out. I want to stay here and wallow, fester in the aftermath of my stupidity.

"Angel will be fine. I will find her. She will be home soon." She tries to touch me.

I fly at her, my face in her face. I am screaming.

"That's ridiculous! You won't find her. You cannot promise me this. You can't solve this. Your family is weird. They have caused me nothing but bother. Leave me alone. We are paying the price for your Mother's abandonment, for her mistakes. He thinks this is normal. He can't have children. He hates women. He has a grudge, so he's kidnapped my Angel. I will find her. I'll find him. I'll kill him."

Winnie turns and walks to the sink. She fills a pint glass with water; hands it to me.

"Drink," She demands.

I take the glass and I fling it right across the van. Liquid sprays onto the dusty surfaces, trickles of dirty water drip down. The glass falls onto the table, soaks your drawings.

"Look what you've done. You came here to upset me." I pick up the sodden pages.

"This is all I have left. You have destroyed them. You are destroying me, my life. Get out get out get out!"

She sits, cross-legged on the floor.

"It's good to get angry. Let it out."

"Oh you and your platitudes, you lot don't live in the real world. Everything I love is gone."

The precious scribblings are dripping.

"Mary," she says. The calmness is now frustrating me, "I love my brother. I trust him. I know he will do the right thing. He knows by now he has made a mistake. He will be trying to correct it. He won't run for long. He will go south. I have an idea where he is. We have friends in Devon who will shelter him. I think he may be there."

"Now you tell me. What friends?"

I could push her, maul her, pick her up and toss her about, shaking information of your location out of her. I want to show her my hurt. I could bundle it all, package it, tie a great big bow around it and hurl it at her, hurt her with it. I could give her my aching muscles, my pounding head, the weight in my chest. I could make her take it all. Make it hers instead of mine.

"The same friends who watched you play your lyre while your Mother and her lover fingered each other?"

I have her attention. New information transforms her face as her brain assimilates it.

"I saw you. I saw you pass the dildo to your Mother. I should have run far, far away from here then. I should have known, a whole other bunch of weirdies have my daughter. Is this a cult? Maybe this is all planned? This is what you people do. I thought your brother would make a good Father. I was wrong, very, very, wrong."

Clawing. Gnawing. Fingers on teeth. Bone on bone. Steaming pressure cooker inside my chest. Something screaming. Deep inside. Around my heart. Take the knife. Stab at it. Cut it out. Make a hole for the hurt, the anger to escape. Too long inside, it has bubbled. Will explode. Flowing from my eyes only in pathetic streams. Women's water drops. Futile furrows in brow now. Mouth a tight, tight line. I should have known better. I should not have secreted you out here, removed you from your friends, your family. It wasn't right, just you and me and the dog. It wasn't fair.

I kept all your kisses and cuddles. Selfishly stole them all. Fed off your love. The simple, honest, childish adoration. I lapped it up. Now my heart will leap out of my bursting chest.

I miss you. I miss the love. The soft little hand stretched out to touch my hair; the smile that lit my life, lighted my world, is blighted now by loneliness. You are lost.

Finally, she rises, unfurls her long legs. She marches to the sink, fills two glasses with water, brings them to me.

"Throw them if you want, but you really need to drink. You don't know what you are saying. You are toxic and confused. Or maybe you want to hurt me? Maybe you want to project your anger onto me?"

Oh insightful and annoying woman!

I grasp a glass, turn away so she cannot see, and drink from it. It is refreshing. It cools my mouth, then my head.

"I am going now. Drink, Mary. Get out in Nature. Eat and keep warm. I will find them. That is my promise to you."

The caravan door clicks shut.

* * *

Weave green willow and red all about and over my head. Let me be dead. Let me not live this life without you.

It is dusty down here on the floor. She hunkers down, her knees click. Her long skirt is gathered in under her. Soon we are both prone on the dusty rotting floor of her Mother's spare caravan. It is the way she touches me. I feel the passion in her fingertips. The touch of her hand on my bare shoulder distracts me. It is a distraction from despair. It is the opposite of despair. I want to wallow in the pit of my own self pity. I have lain here all night, telling myself I am useless and deserve only death.

She runs her hand over my shoulder, kneads my muscle, pushes fingers into flesh, releases, tugs instead at my hair; drags my face round to hers.

"There is news. It is good. He is in Devon. They were seen on the high street in Totnes. Our community spreads far. I will go. Your daughter will be fine".

Her hand is as delicate as tissue paper floating on my skin. It leaves a gooseflesh of gossamer. My hair is smoothed away from my face. The same way I tuck a curl behind your ear; to see you more clearly. I stand to accuse her of something.

"You said you would find them, you said this last week."

My words are like chicken slops thrown out in a strong breeze. Long limbs stretch to contain the flurry. Eyes bore deep within my skull, searching for a clue, assessing my mental health. She shakes out her head. Curls fall to the conversation.

"You hold so much anger in your body".

"Are you surprised given the circumstances?"

The desperation of death is the only answer.

She chews her bottom lip, twirls the curl.

"Mary, he won't harm her. Focus on light. She'll be having an adventure. But you must know that already or else you would have asked about how she was."

Death, or perhaps a heart attack or a stroke induced by shock; like my Father.

"What do you mean, I haven't asked about her?"

"You haven't. You have only worried about yourself; how you miss her. She may be having quite a nice holiday. My brother will spoil her. She'll have her own bed, maybe her own room, probably in a nice house with an indoor toilet. She'll be able to have a bath every night."

My Father was silenced after a secret was told. Kaku and the People of The Rocks come for me now. There is too much feeling in my heart. I cannot cope with more. I have been tested, pushed to the limit of myself. I cannot go on. An imaginary snowdrop will never ease this futility I feel. Rock people take me to be as rock. Please.

My Mother, the day we fished her car out of Loch Tay. I have been moored to a rock. I cemented my feet to a concrete captor. Hands at my throat, hovering; making heat.

"Your throat chakra is all out of shape. It needs to be balanced. Then you may say what you feel is appropriate, it will be easier."

I cannot escape the cords, linked patterns of learnt behaviour, my bondage. The terrible thing I brought to my Parents house. The truth that drove us apart. The other girl I loved, long ago when I was just twenty, her black hair and green eyes.

The chaos my heart made of love. The confusion then; the desperate wanting and never having. And then, the decision made, that love would always be elusive to me. I steered my soul away from the thing it wanted. I denied it. I did.

"Come out. We shall go for a walk. It is good to be out in Nature. We get comfort from the beauty of the planet. It is easier to understand our fate when faced with the magnificence of our Maker".

"This is not my fate. I don't want to understand it. I want to go to the Police. Your brother took my child. This is kidnapping. He is disturbed. Why are you protecting him?"

"This is nothing. Nothing really matters. Reality's just in your head."

"Bring me my child back or I go to the Police."

There is blankness in both of her eyes now. She stares off into nothingness.

"We both know that the Police will not listen. They will not believe you. He has been too clever. You have made Walter her legal guardian. You are too irrational. This has to have its' own timing needs to be handled differently, approached with love. Learn the lesson. Witness that which brought you here. It is all inside you."

It is a melancholy acceptance. Her facts displayed as wisdom.

"What do you know about it?"

"Mary, I know everything about it!"

The arms make that fluttering motion again. She's thinking about hugging me so that we bond. I want only you to hold, only to hug you. But, she does, she wraps herself about me, holds me close and tight, her tiny breasts in my chest. Her heart beating, mine a-thumping. She whispers in my ear, short shallow breaths followed by sighs. Her mouth quivers. Honesty.

"My Father was rarely around. I yearned for him for all my life. My Mother was crazier than she is now. We lived in Holland."

She steps away from me. But I am left in that moment of her holding me. She takes her coat, hands me mine. She opens the door for me.

I go out with her. She babbles morsels of hurt; low and broken bits of sentences. Her Mother felt trapped in the conservative society.

"Grand Mother told us, at bed time most nights, she told us how we lost our Mamma."

Every few feet we stop to examine. The forest enthrals her; she kicks at the crunchy leaves, touches a tree petrified by ice. Birds get blessed. The Mother's stories differ.

"It was Grand Mother's order that sent her to Scotland. She came to retrieve her husband but met Elsie instead. It was Elsie or us."

Monstrous bed time tales tell of Grand Mothers' cruelty.

"We felt abandoned, betrayed by her. I visited them. He didn't, wouldn't."

Respect for her Mother grew. Gertrude's drive to stand in truth awed her. Grand Mother is revealed now as a furious woman only ever relaxed when in control of others. Pockets are emptied of scraps to feed foxes or rats. I see him as a boy. I want to hate her. Her kindness maddens me. Every living thing is honoured. My head turns this way, that way; constantly looking, searching for the one that is missing. Geese prepare to leave, call and cry for their children while fat herons balance.

You.

I go to the wood, to the hammock. The days spent clambering this old rope haunt the place. I lie down. It is impossible to settle.

"Relax," she says. The hand comes to me again. The fishing net lurches as I leave. I stand to one side, hands on hips. A movement catches me. I crouch down to embrace you. You do not come. Woof appears to lick my hands, my face.

Shudders of life before you cause a hot panic. All my terrible times are lodged in my throat.

She sees.

There is no other way. My hand is greedy. My touch has a little more force. Against the airy piano fingers I am clod of earth. On the lonely lips I show a little of the tiger. I have the handle at her hip, thumb the roll; move her to me. First there is shock but it goes. The chiselled jaw is the same as his, but it is softer, softer in the palm of my hand and softer still on my tongue, more responsive. I take her hand, nervously at first; I lead her down to the water. There are silver birch trees at the river and against one of them she leans, backs into it waiting. These great spades more used to digging than caressing find her bones under clothes. Soft flesh at her hip. I touch her lips with mine, she thrusts her tongue into my mouth, in much the same way her brother did, but she has passion in her heart, transfers that to me and I quiver. I kiss her eyes. I blow soft breaths in her ear, let a low moan echo inside her head.

"I want you." I say.

I bend to the boots and unlace them, put the socks inside them. I help her out through the trees and into the river, onto a rock made for two. We sit and winter pinkens the too-blue sky.

Her eyes are like those of the tiger, green and deep and true. Into them and into the water I go. Knee deep but anchored.

Fixed and focused. Where are you? How are you? When will I see you, hold you again? I remove her raggedy old jumper; peel the layers until soft round breasts give up their nipples. Rosehips dangle over clear water. Scarlet droplets. Tempting. Small birds watch.

I hold her nipples with the tips of my fingers.

"I enjoyed your Dance," she tells me. "We all saw the tiger on the top of the totem. Only I know it was you."

Without a tremor she speaks. Her eyes aglow.

Lapping river water makes her shiver. I hold her. There's a natural force makes her want to love little birds and golden leaves. A breathing heart with no home. A rootless tree. I cannot add to it. Harm no living thing. I smooth it out, knead the knots in shoulders; spread my hands all about her skin. She is frozen here on this rock with her feet in the water and her jumper slung onto the bank. I warm her. Further down on the rock and towards me her hips find mine. She clings, with legs wrapped. Thin legged, knickerless hippy. Here's the girl Wallace calls 'sister'. A woman who scatters her frail feelings onto rooks and ravens and crows, calls them all brother without judgement. Anthropomorphic soul. The watcher and hand maiden, helper, facilitator. Her lifetime of silence cannot now be undone. Through childhood and up to this moment she has waited for one who was stronger. Someone who would say, speak, fight. There is a beautiful woman with her bare legs wrapped around me, desperate for help, trapped on one path, another beckoning. I know that need for release.

The tendon in the groin, the protruding line like an arrow that is absent in men, I run my finger along it, feel the sharp edges jut from the inside of her thigh. I lower my head, my lips. Dip into the hollows either side. She stretches out on the rock.

A sheep bleats nearby. Woof has disappeared. A stag leads his girls to the water's edge. We watch them drink.

I have known this woman since the first moment he came into my home. He has spoken of her in almost every sentence. I have seen her pass the ancient dildo to her Mother. I have been tended by her in ceremony. This woman with few words sees all, knows all and yet cannot break the family silence. She knows where he is. Only this one can communicate with him.

Her skirt is in the water. She lies back on the rock, dips her hands into the cold, grabs clumps of my hair. I have no dildo, nor anything like it; this is no fancy ceremony calling unseen goddesses to book. This is my fight for my daughter. How do I find you? Where do I begin? Too fiercely I pull at her, needing more, much more than truth now. This terrible tongue finds the place, finds where the truth lies, hidden away. Taste and flick. I watch her move.

She unbuckles my belt. She takes the waistband of my jeans and pulls me down on top of her. My face above her face. The taste of her sex on my tongue. She raises her feet and hooks them into the top of my jeans, pulls them down, runs one foot between my legs, pushing in, pushing in. One leg now around my waist. Again she thrusts her mouth to mine. I forget everything. My stomach jumps. My heart soars. I have never been kissed like this.

Her thumb is inside me, moving back and forth, pressing against my walls, rubbing me up and down, in and out. It is exquisite. I stare into her eyes, bewildered. Her mouth hangs open. Her eyes are aflame. She kisses every part of my face. And then she fills me. Curls the hand and fills me with it. Has me. Owns me. And she rocks her whole beating, beautiful body inside me and I can feel every movement. Her passion for me pulses through me. I can only stand there, in the river, with my jeans and my pants all about my ankles and the cold water running along the backs of my legs and allow myself to be lost in this one perfect incredible moment. And I have to cling to her as I come. Deep and loud, I call to the wild, to the wildness in all of us and I hear my voice but I cannot control it. I cannot stop.

Frozen on this rock, laid, stretched like a white stick caught while free birds hop from bough to bough. I look up from her long thighs through the branches. The Golden eagle also circles. Hips and birds go round and round and life plays memories like movies. The drum beat of circle dancing. Endless concentric infinities. Eagle screeches.

The day I silenced my Father forever. The reason my Mother drove the car into the loch. I silenced and shocked them. Said I might be gay. Their shame. Their shame. He never spoke again. She sips gin without a cherry.

But now, years later, I stand in a river in my own truth, this gentle soul to touch. I remember the day your Daddy left. When his shock and repulsion turned love sour. I told him my babe, I told him too. The lie I have lived was whispered blushed with romance. I admitted it. My shame, my shame.

And then I feel it, deep within me. Tapping at courage; the courage to love; to love myself. The humility of honesty makes us vulnerable and beautiful. Hidden instincts massaged, honoured.

"This isn't your first time," she says.

"Or yours," I reply.

"Our family has a gay gene," she giggles "we must honour it or end up like Granny."

Our cries frighten the deer and they run. Let me Live. Let me

Live. I hear her moan. I feel her shudder, hot breath in gasps. We freeze and scream it all out. I see you dance into adulthood. A tiny speck of fear before my eyes. Outwith my grasp. Without me.

"How do I find my daughter?"

"Mother will have to take some responsibility for him this time."

"This time? This time? Elsie said that. He's done this before?"

One leaf sweeps down past her head, is caught on the silk of a spider, swings, twirls above her; just hangs there, suspended by an unseen force.

Spider webs – I broke the fast. I cheated. This is my punishment. The leaf twirls on its invisible thread. I wait to watch it drop. The twin cannot find an answer. There is a truth to be shared. In one truth there are many twists. I wait, with questions.

"Answer me. Has he done this before?" I have to pant. My breath has been taken. I have to focus, remember. I had forgotten you. For a moment all I knew was her.

"Yes."

The filigree net with its glistening dew is caught still down the back of my mouth. The terrible drought I felt returns. I have to stare squarely at her. I do not want to look at her. The transparency shimmers; the way there's no filter twixt eye and heart. I have to understand; have to listen although it is hard.

"Go on," I whisper.

"He took me away when we were ten. He saved the change our Grand Mother gave him. He forged papers, bribed an older kid and we flew to Glasgow. He thought our Father was there. We stayed with his relatives. They phoned Mother, we had a nice vacation then we went home to Grand Mother. It has not been spoken about again."

"It is not his fault. He wants Mother's attention. He has questions. He does not understand as I do. He is not quite grown up; often thinks as a small boy would. It is terrible for you but I will promise you Angel will be fine."

"The last time he did this, he was asked to babysit my ex-partner's little boy. They were gone for six months. He visited our Father. He tried to pass the child off as his own. Naturally my relationship broke down. Elsie and I agree that Mother will have to do something now. She will have to be honest with him in a way he can comprehend. But it's difficult. He was such a lost soul without her, when he was a boy. He clung to me. He cried all the time. She doesn't know that. He'll break down in front of her if the subject is mentioned."

Words as waves: the sounds of the lives of other people wash me. The terrible burdens we carry, splashes of sadness. I am as one wave in this great ocean of lives and loves. Everything I need is already inside of me. The lesson is clear. Truth will out. This time he is cleverer. But I will not wait another week. I will not have another week without you.

"Help me, please," I whisper kisses.

"I will drive to Devon in the morning. We have links to an intentional community there. It's best if you stay here. I'll give you a spare mobile and you can phone me anytime. I'll text you, too. This is just a test. Walter is no Paedophile. Have you enough food in the van? You can go up to the house you know."

Lives and loves. Hurts and misdemeanours. Right and wrong. Black and white.

She takes me by the hand back to the van, through the raised beds, passed the compost toilet. We dry in front of the stove.

I throw sodden clothes outside. I fall into bed. She covers me with a duvet and blankets. The door clicks shut. I sleep. You come and cuddle me, tell me you are fine, tell me you have been to a swimming pool. I am whole.

Many hours later the mobile rings. It is she. It is morning.

"How are you? Were you asleep? I had a wonderful time yesterday. I think you are wonderful, even with all this stress, these tense times, you show such love and tenderness. I am missing you, but getting ready for the journey. I will go after lunch. There's no news yet. I'll speak later."

I breathe. Inhale. Exhale.

"You are beautiful." I say. "I want you. But you must get ready. Text me later. I was asleep."

She hangs up. There's a large glass of water by my bed. The robin came in to look for food. Fallen rainbows drip into muddy puddles. I sip. The tin cage has many fine views. The wind lashes at the sea. I pace and jump to keep warm, bend to the stove, stretch again, then once lit I lie in front of it with my book. The book I have kept in my wooden chest.

I write 'Winnie thinks you have a better life with him.'

Expansive bathrooms. Flush toilets. Your own bed. Pretty dresses. Glossy encyclopaedias. Fromage frais.

The other scene plays over in my mind. The day my Mother moved away from the stench of her failure. The guilt burned, and burns now. A plan borne of shame turns russet in my belly.

I run up the track. I know I have to convince her to help me. The book is full of lists: How to Lose Your Daughter. I invited him in, fucked him in the wet, mid morning as you snoozed. You are mine. But I allowed you to go. I climb into her car.

"I have a plan," she says, "Mother and Elsie and I forged a plan last night. We stayed up talking all night. We spoke with respect. There was no need for hurt or accusation. I will get him, stay with him; explain. Mother will speak with him. She has promised to use all the tenderness she has, to reassure him over the phone, that all is well, that time will heal, that she will take care of him, that she loves him, despite everything. Then she will follow me down south in a few days, when he is less defensive, when he has begun to accept that his behaviour is unacceptable."

"Let me drive," I say. "I want to come with you."

And she does. She clambers over to the passenger seat, tucks an old tartan rug around her and programmes the sat nav for me.

"There are epiphanies in your eyes," she says and falls asleep. The road is empty, just an early stag with frosty antlers. We are travellers of any age on any quest, like Sioux returning from the Winter Lands. Eagle country is a vast bog with a well worn track.

Deep instinct tells me you are fine. The Motherhood button, pressed three years ago beeps reassurances but sends stunning thudders. Separation from kin, from love, is constant.

I touch her many times. I want to. When she sleeps I run my finger along her jaw, put my hand on her head. When she wakes I grasp the inside of her thigh, make conversation.

"I did not know whether or not to contact her Father. In the end I didn't."

"It may not be the right time."

A shift pattern emerges. We say little and the radio doesn't work. One sleeps and the other drives. Motorways numb. Times I fought for love and lost. This I win.

12

WHOLE

I am here. I am Here. Reach out. Reach out always. I have taken my eyes off you. But that is all.

She and I sleep on a couch at her friend's house. We wrap our bodies together. We hold each other through the night. If she turns, I turn with her. She talks and worries about her brother.

At 9am we are outside his house. I see you when the door opens, each footfall soft, each movement measured I reach for you.

"Mamma, where you been?"

And that is it. You are in my arms, and I am whole. The world revolves again, correctly on its axis. I kiss you. I kiss her. I hold you both to me. This is it. This is my whole world, my happiness.

At 9.15am the mobile rings. I pass it to him.

"Hello," he says.

"I am sorry, son," she says.

I leave him as they speak.

"Blessings on the telephone bill," says Winnie.

She takes my place.

For a while we watch one mother's children sob for secrets

revealed. Our dog, in her new red collar, needs a walk.

"Mammy, come and see the swings."

We leave them. I look at her and she looks at me, small smiles on our lips, deep, deep longing on our hips.

You, me and the dog go to the play park.

* * *

Mothers and fathers mingle. They wear cottons and linens; hand died cloth; hand made brogues. This is the organic brigade, unhealthy looking vegetarians who are too thin; too pure.

You dig in a sand pit; run to the slide, whiz and chase around amongst all the pre-schoolers, children that are younger than you. You dig and dig. Woof beats that long black tail 'til it is nearly broke. I sit on the bench. There's a steady stream of carrot-wielding carers. We watch our offspring. A two-year-old boy delights in flinging sand at other children's eyes. You cry as your eyes sting. The parent smiles adoringly, seemingly unaware that she should stop him. Politeness prevents her intervention. I lean into the other woman.

"Mind your child," I say. I go over and pick you up in my arms, wiping the sand away, kissing it better. I hug you too tight. I point to the see-saw and the other small girl waiting for a playmate. You run off.

I kneel down and look at the wee boy.

"Don't throw sand." I tell him.

The Mother watches me. I do not react. I do not fling sand in her eyes. I do not claw at her. The Bengal Tiger rests inside me. I return to the picnic bench. I watch your every move, from see-saw to roundabout, up the climbing frame, our brown eyes meet, and they shine. You skip back to me, into my arms and away again to giggle with the girls.

The boy's mother is Andrea. She stays a while and we chat. She produces a picnic of miniature organic rice cakes and goats' cheese. She made the hummus herself. She tells me of her recent departure from computer systems analysis to part time adult literacy. She has downsized her life in order to show young Henry that money is not everything in life. She describes to me the process of growing vegetables. I nod. She advises me on recycling. I listen. She has forsaken her sports car for a bicycle. She has a special trailer for Henry and the shopping. It is five miles from the town to their farmhouse. She hopes her husband will agree to work from home next year.

"We live on an island off the north west coast of Scotland, hundreds of miles from Edinburgh or Glasgow. There are no big shops. We have been living in a caravan on a farm for about a year. There was no toilet. I made one from pallets. I dug a great big hole then built a shed around it. When we use the toilet we throw herbs and dried flowers into the pit. I planted willow beds to soak up the effluent. We catch fish from the rocks. I grow salads and vegetables. My landlady has hens for eggs, goats for milk and cheese. We eat venison the old farmers shoot. Poachers give us salmon and rabbit. We barter scallops and mussels."

The romance of my life fills her with longing.

Time passes and parents change. There is a conveyor belt of non-consumers. We are included in every picnic. I have no food to share. I have no money in my pocket. I do not know where the nearest shop is. You bounce back and forth from swing to picnic bench. You taste the delights of Devon. They sit and laud their green credentials, open-handed with their food, well-mannered folk.

I speak of the mountains. I tell them about the wild hills of heather and moss where deer and eagles have their homes. The shapes that land can make, the light that changes everything.

"Do you remember our hills?" I ask you.

"We gonna live here now?" You ask.

"No, we don't live here, we are just on holiday."

She comes then with the sun at her back, my thin hippy. She sways gently. On her lips are my kisses. I am starving for them. I excuse myself from the group of women, and I go to my kisses. I take them. In this cosmopolitan world I can touch her.

"Hello! I am pleased to see you too." She says.

"You look much better. The Angel seems happy and un-scathed. He knows he has done wrong. He is still crying. The tears of a lifetime have only begun to fall. But it is the beginning of his healing. Mum is crying too. She is sorry she left him. She understands she should never have left us. It will take some time, Mary. Mum will come here. We have so much to talk about. So many years we have been silent with each other. We have closed down our hearts because it was always too painful to say the things we needed to. Now, because of what he has done. We have no choice. I know how awful it is. But you have helped us. Because of your suffering we will be a proper family again. You should go and move out of the caravan. I will miss you but I must help my family and you must process all that has happened. It is the only way. I do not want to see you go. Go home Mary. Don't stay here. I will be back. I will look for you and from now until then I will miss you terribly."

She leans into me, her head on my chest, her hair falling about all over my arms. I hold her to me, brush my cheek on top of her head, smelling her, then my fingers stroke the nape of her neck. I feel her throb gently, her breath becomes shallow and she must compose herself, here in the play park after all that has happened.

"You will need the bus keys," she says. She is staying strong and focused. "The tank is full of diesel. I have put credit on your mobile. I took five hundred pounds from Walter's wallet. Here it is. Mum is coming down to get him. She has been shamed and she is angry. It is good."

She is my rock.

"I made a list. Here are the things that you have to do. I have already telephoned the social worker. He gave me the name, said he lied, told the social worker he lied, told them what he had done. It is important for him to finally know honesty. This is just a journey Mary. This is how we learn. You too must find honesty. You must find your truth and stand proud in it. There is no shame in wanting me; there is no shame in what we have done. We are grown women, consenting adults. I think you are beautiful. I will miss you and I hope to see you again."

She gives me my book. She has written in it. From another vantage point she has seen a way.

You come to her without questions. You wrap two arms about her leg. She smiles and bends down to you.

"It's time to go home baby," She says, "You have a new adventure waiting. I will see you when you are bigger."

We look at each other without a forecast to the future. We do not know what will happen. We do not know if we will ever meet again. I glance at her list, the actions she thinks I must take. Then, I reach out with my hands and I take her face. I breathe along her eyebrows and sniff at her ears. My cheek rubs into her hair and, breast to soft breast, we hold each other.

"I would like to see you again." I say.

"When you have both recovered, when you are settled again.

We know our timing is terrible. You must keep the bus. I must help Mum and Walter."

"I will find a new way. I will find my own way. Then I will text you." I say.

She kisses me. Her tongue sweeps into my mouth, filling me. Her pelvis grinds into mine. Mothers and children chat and play. You sing about Marjory Daw on a see-saw. She walks back into the sun.

I look again at the list. This woman has understood, all that I implied. Everything I cried, she took. Her first suggestion is perfect. We must move. Of course you and I must go from the caravan. Too much has happened there, and none of it was good for you. We must live in a town, near a school and other children. I cannot segregate you; keep you as closeted as I have been.

But, there is something she has forgotten. There is one thing she has no knowledge of – Winnie has no insight into Motherhood. Her practical advice excludes your needs. You need me. You only need your Mother to be there and be happy. I failed you when I took my eyes off you.

13

OF ROAD AND ROCK

We see now the little terraced houses. Parallel and perpendicular to each other. Mile on mile. Row on row. Lanes to play in. From here to the horizon. Brick alleys run in and out of light. They are decorated with shopping trolleys, crisp packets. Plastic bags meet in corners.

We walk through. I need to be sure. Down the High Street we avoid the broken glass. We smile and I nod because that is what we are used to doing. They do not smile back. The locals pass by. They do not nod. They do not smile. In the Bakers I ask a thin woman for a Bridie. She curls her lip at me. I am a fool for asking. There are many pies. Dozens of different pastries filled with meat or cheese. I need the particular pleasure of a Forfar Bridie. Mince and onions and flaky pastry. I could settle for a Scotch pie. But she does not sell them. Stress and lack of sleep catch me. Unfamiliar English tastes unsettle me. I may cry. The taste of home has flung itself on me in the guise of a snack. I order six sausage rolls. Two each. I do not nod or smile at any one again. We just go back to the bus to eat. I check the map and decide to go north.

You fall asleep in the crumbs. Woof hoovers the mess. At forty miles an hour we chug. My mind wanders. I remember our situation; try to make some sense of it.

We are homeless. There is nowhere for us to go. You and I have nowhere to live. Our belongings are stored in a shed on a croft on a Scottish island. Our few clothes are in a caravan that we really cannot live in any more. We cannot stay there. I have screwed the son, played with his mind. I have stolen knowledge from the Mother. But I may have given the daughter a piece of my heart.

That is all it takes. One fleeting thought of her and I am useless for all other rational sensible practical purposes. Instead of planning how to extract your toys and teddies from the croft, I am luxuriating in the softness of her skin. It is pale skin. Pale and silky. Smooth to my touch. Her eyes flash when I touch her. She lights inside. Her breasts fit just so into my mouth. Her eyes listen, offering the wisdom older women weep for. Deep desire rises inside me; to run my finger down her spine and watch her shudder, to tickle the curve of her breast until the corners of her mouth lift. To let my tongue taste just once more the very essence of her. But, she has written in my book. Advice for leaving the croft. Ways to leave them and let them heal. Her hand writing. Her notes. This is what she wants. Maybe, she is just like her twin and likes the thrill of a brief encounter with a vulnerable woman. Maybe I used her to find him. To find you.

The first time I saw her was in Ceremony. She was dancing, swaying, skipping barefoot in a willow bender. She plucked the music of sex from a lyre; she held her Mother's great dildo aloft and I was transfixed. I wanted her then.

I have kissed every inch of her. The masses of curls have trailed all over me, springs tickling. I have run my tongue the length of her. She has watched over me, brought me food, taken care of me. She has wiped an ocean of tears from my cheeks, kissed me; tasted me. Those butterfly hands have been deep inside me. True green orbs locked into mine, we stayed staring into each other often for hours. Nose to nose, lips to lips, tongue on tongue.

And yet I drive away. I drive north and northwest. I must go back to her Mother's croft, to remove myself, ultimately, from her life. My stomach needs to empty itself at the prospect. My bowels heave and loosen. Map in hand. Fumes from cars, lorries, my new bus. Here we are again. Back in the bus. You are all cosied up with a banana and a bag of Doritos. Woof watches out the windows, alert. The road stretches before us like the greatest greyest ribbon. I do not know where we will go. There is an inkling of a notion that city life may appeal to us. Procrastination borne of indecision makes me drive on the small roads, so that I can wander in and out of towns and villages. I want to see what I may be missing. I want to know if we can live here. There are shops and play parks. There are cultured Mammies. The glorious galleries will be hiding around here somewhere. It was my dream, before the world changed, to live in a little terraced house with a Tesco and a Jungle Gym nearby. She is here, somewhere, she knows this area, has some semblance of a life here. I am torn. Ripped inside.

Gertrude's phrases fill my head. 'Trust the Universe' stings my eyes like the awful lemon and herb cleaning solution. 'Stand in your own Truth' revolves before me like a disco ball, mirrored realities of all shapes and colours circling, no way to know which one will settle, which version of reality is true and real. The ways of my heart and the ways of my world play havoc with all I had thought I had learned. My ego is but an encumbrance. Society's rules are out dated. The constraints that bind me must be broken. I must relinquish all I thought I knew, must die to self, she said. It is important to lose all I hold dear. The possessions and people that we gather around us must be removed. We cannot hold onto anything in this world. We must not. We must free ourselves of everything so that we may bring only light to our hearts and bodies and therefore the planet. These were Gert's words. Winnie understood them. I need some grasp of the concept the wise women advocate.

I lost you. I lost our home. I have lost all our clothes and belongings. I lost my Mother and Father; my family home. I lost my career. And now, I have lost my lover.

I may search and search for my missing parts. The simple truths of my heart that make me whole.

Massive chimneys touch the sky. Black smoke belches into cloud. Signs offer Services and IKEA. I turn off the motorway.

Back home, on the island, there are crofts smaller than this car park. Whole families, generations of the same family, can farm a stretch of land a fraction of the size of this place and sustain body and soul in the process. I take good note of where I leave the bus, though there is little need. There is no other vehicle like it anywhere near. There are large shiny new BMW's and people carriers and four wheel drive's.

IKEA is a revelation. It is an aircraft hangar full to the rafters with stuff. We follow the painted line along with other dutiful shoppers. I push you in a trolley. We go round and round. I examine all the pretty fleecy blankets, the different coloured lamps and lamp shades. Rugs and shelves. From floor to ceiling there are Things. And it is all so cheap and so accessible. I can afford to shop here. I can load this trolley with some of this stuff. I can replace the stuff I lost. I can buy and buy. I can spend the money Winnie gave me. But my head spins. My breath becomes shallow. I begin to feel dizzy and cannot breathe. There is too much choice. We have to go.

I could spend and spend and never have the thing I desire. I could fill the gap in my life with neoprene kitchen accessories in green or red or blue. But I only want you and her and woof and me to be together. I have never felt alone before, have not ever touched the concept of loneliness. I felt apart, felt marginalised at times in my life. I have felt disillusioned with my world, at odds with the rules and the norms. But not simply because IKEA frightens me. This is not the life for us. We need fresh air, mountains covered in heather. We have choices again.

We could brum the dusty roads. We could shelter in the hedge rows. We could live a life of freedom and adventure; finding bits of work, foraging and living as nomads. The temptation to run away in this mini bus is overwhelming. To drive forever. I can see us venturing farther, seeing more. You could observe the lives of many different cultures, of many a fine place. You could be a little citizen of the world and I your own tour guide.

You and me and the dog on the motorways of England. I drive again. I pass the chimneys, the factories, the vast shopping complexes. I have no interest in them. They are not part of me or my world. It is easy to discard the surplus stuff. All this is inconsequential, a mere distraction to my heart and the journey of truth I find myself on. I search instead for something of substance, something with purpose and meaning. Or something familiar and comfortable. I want to lie down and cry and feel safe. There must be a place in this world that speaks with my heart. As you do.

I don't stop until I reach home. I drive us to Stirling then around the Wallace Monument, passed the battlegrounds and the Castle. You sleep and so avoid my history lessons. Another time, I say aloud. We will be here again. Someday I will tell you all about the great heroes of Scotland. Of William Wallace and the men who yearned to emulate him. There will be tales too of the man who called himself Wallace, who stole you away to England and how Mammy rescued you from the land of shops and chimneys. Maybe we will laugh. Maybe we will learn. We will learn to stay together, to look after each other. To be content. I park in Dobie's garden centre to pee. And then we go again. Callandar is quiet. I keep driving, eyes stinging, squinting through the dark. We are going home. Home. The old farm house in Fearnan. Loch Tay sleeps. And there it is. Lights shine from my old family home. I have not been back here for several years, but I know the house is rented out. I do not know the tenants. There is no reason for me to ring the bell. I should not. I cannot simply waltz in and demand shelter. We will camp. We have to. We will have a fire outside and watch the stars. I park in a field next to some standing stones. We gather wood for a fire and we sit among the shadows, looking up into the stars. I tell you a story of the stars.

Irky and Oompi were lovers. They sat in the sky and shone for each other. Centuries of smiling light, night after night. Side by side they glittered. One night a fast comet came and knocked them apart. They fell out of their orbit and away from each other. Down down down they fell to Earth. Their lights were shattered. Scattered a hundred million times all over this planet. Tiny shards of the brightest sparks fell into the people and the animals. Each one of us has a tiny piece of a star inside, to help us glow. We come from Light, my Angel. We Love and we love forever and ever. I will love you for centuries and even when we are apart I will love you.

Moon, stars and fire bounce off ancient rock. I have known these Stones all of my life. My own Mother and I would lie here in troubled times. She would sing and I would watch. And, as I have learned, so do I teach. I hum the air, raise the notes in my throat and let my voice sing the songs of childhood. I skip around this friendly old boulder, take you by the hand and we laugh and we giggle. The dog shakes her ears. Shooting stars burst above us. I wish and I wish. I wish my Mother was here to help me. I wish Winnie was here to kiss and hold me. I wish I knew what to do next. I wish I had a Scotch pie or a Forfar Bridie. Exhausted, you fall asleep and I lay you down on the back seat of the bus. I go back outside and lie on the earth. A sliver of a new moon keeps my eyes looking Heavenward. I lie beside the fire. It is not warm. I dream of her warm arms, the safety I felt wrapped together in the caravan. I pray for a way back into those arms.

This was my first rock. The first lessons I learnt in strength. I lie down as my Mother used to; along the face of it so my body is almost shielded.

"No one can harm a rock" she used to say.

We would make rock faces, my Mother and I; pretending we were stone and impassive. Pretending we could not get hurt. I was a teenager then. The hormones of a first crush like dervishes caged. She knew and she was afraid for me. Afraid of the difficulties ahead.

"This is the face you must wear, Mary." She said. "Never let anyone know how you feel or what you're thinking. That's how they get in, you see; get inside your heart and cause you the pain of the heart. That'll hurt you Mary, the pain in the heart is a terrible thing. Be like a rock Mary. Be a rock. I fell in love with him. With your Father. He came to my village very fortnight for work. He sought me out and he seduced me with fine talk. I was a naïve Irish girl. I was seventeen, just out of school and not much older than you are now. I was bored in my wee village; wanted away. And I ran off and married him without thinking at all. Before I had the sense to know who I was or what I wanted. I married him and he brought me here. I thank God each morning and night for you. I thank this rock for the strength to continue."

Sinking deeper. Words I didn't heed.

I am rock. Hard. Impenetrable. I have been thrust from the Earth's core.

I am Earth. Musty, soft, fertile. I am a source of life and heat.

I am fire. Aflame in my life. A beacon burning. Extinguishable by water.

Flowing, pouring, running water. Gushing. I am sinking deeper, deeper, deeper. Sobbing, begging. I beg the elements to take me now. I sob and sob and beg for forgiveness. I am a failure. I am a burden. I have not respected love or life. Please help me. We have nothing. No home, no family, no work. We very nearly lost each other.

Tears flowing, flooding cheek and hair. Rushing out. Needing to be free.

14

THE BREATH OF HISTORY

I am starving. I am hungry for her touch; I am hungry for her company. A piece of me is gone and I am empty. I need to be filled. She filled me with her hand. She filled my life. I am complete with her around. This I know and yet cannot act upon, cannot feel this way, must not allow myself to be distracted by anyone but you.

You. You climb around the rocks, poke fingers in cup marks. You chase woof; lie on top of her, check her ears for goodness knows what.

"My Woof," you say.

"Bestest Woof."

She licks you, washes your face for you. She sticks her nose into your hair and snuffles; blows down her nose, shakes her head and, of course, wags her tail tirelessly.

"C'mon," I tell you both, "We'll go and get some breakfast. I know a place, I think."

Scottish pastries are the best. I still hanker for one. Thick and juicy – I may try to feed the hole she left, stuff my face with spicy mince and forget I ever met her.

The Bakery is still there, a childhood landmark.

"A scrambled egg roll, three Bridie's, three Scotch pies, a

carton of apple juice, soup and a coffee please." I say.

"I'll get you a wee box for all that lot," says the round girl behind the counter.

"…Oh, and a couple of sausage rolls and some millionaire's shortbread," I add.

I carry the box like a trophy. I nod to the old wifies on the street. They nod back. We chat about the weather. Suddenly I am happy. I take you by the hand and skip down the street with you. Then I have a remarkable idea – I decide to introduce you to your Granddad. His nursing home is somewhere nearby.

I eat the pastry in the bus knowing that Walter would be most upset about the mess. One hand on the wheel, the other stuffing food into my face, I forgot the brown sauce. You enjoy the scrambled egg and woof licks the first of the sausage rolls from her lips.

I know the old, converted house. I was here to see my Pappa many years ago. They have built a ramp for wheelchairs since then. We knock and wait. Woof sits on the mat. The door opens. I introduce myself.

"We haven't seen you for a long time," says the nurse, "He's through here. Mind the tubes now. He's been having wee turns every week or so, and we put n that tube in case we needed to feed him. Your Mother has been phoning regularly. Will I tell her you visited?"

"Yes, please do." I reply.

There he is, sitting in a large Parker Knoll armchair in the stinking day room: my dumb and drooling Daddy. Once vibrant and full of his own voice, now unable to speak never mind raise his voice to me. One side of his face has defied gravity it falls out of synch with the rest of his world. An arm lies limp across his lap. A tufty beard shows he has not yet been shaved. His eyes are grey and watery and full of torment. This is the hell he preached about.

"Hi Dad," I say, "Do you remember me?"

He snorts and I realise he knows exactly who I am. The other arm is raised, pulls me to him. He grumbles deep, angry, incomprehensible sounds into my ear. I do not know what he is angry about, whether it is at me or at him, whether this is some sort of greeting or whether he has something of import to impart. Maybe it is a Shakespearean quote.

You fidget. Bored, you look for something to play with. I take the shortbread out of my bag and break a bit off, hand it to you. He holds out his hand. I break another bit off and give it to him.

"This is your granddaughter," I tell him, "Her name is Angel. She's nearly three."

He takes my left hand to look for a wedding ring. Grumbles and dribbles when he cannot see one, or even the hint of a mark of one. He glares as best he can, stuffs the biscuit into his mouth.

"I am single. Her Father left when I was pregnant. I did not want him enough and he knew it. I have raised her alone. We have been living in a caravan but we are homeless just now. I was seeing someone but I don't want to talk about it. Have you seen Mum?"

He turns a little purple. It starts on his nose, in among the hairs and the exposed pores then spreads across his cheeks. You turn to watch, hold out a little hand for more biscuit. We eat and watch him fume. Then he begins to choke. He stops breathing. His lips are purple. His eyes are boggling. The good arm clutches at his throat then at me. He motions me to clap him on the back. I yell for a nurse. I yell and yell and scream for a nurse. I don't really want to touch him. I am afraid he will regain his voice and rant at me for doing it wrong. A lifetime of being told I am wrong has taken its' toll. I stand useless, watching my father choke on Scottish shortbread.

"Did you feed him?" yells the nurse.

"Yes, why?" I ask.

"He's had several strokes. He can't swallow. That's why we put in the tubes. We feed him pureed mash only. I did tell you."

"You did not tell me," I reply. Oh God. I killed my Father.

A carer comes in rolling a suction unit. They stick a long plastic hose into his mouth and extract the food I gave him. He is now only semi-conscious, pale and has to be taken to bed. Someone has gone to telephone an emergency doctor. His next of kin will have to be notified. My Mother has asked to be notified of any change in his condition. They have her mobile number.

"Will you tell my Mother I am here, please?" I ask.

The nurse and the carer wheel my Father away. We sit in the room with the other old people. They are all waiting to die. Some appear jealous that his suffering may be ending quicker than theirs. It is the way they look up and look away again with pleading then sorrow in equal measures. No one speaks. Daytime television has been switched to Jeremy Kyle. Another carer sits with her feet up and a cup of tea; on her break.

You are oblivious. Having lived in close proximity to so many weird and colourful characters, having already seen so many situations develop and resolve themselves, you are growing into a very relaxed, laid back little person.

Soon we are called to the office. The Matron beckons me over and hands me the telephone.

"Mary?" says my Mother. "Mary, what has happened to your poor Daddy?"

Her soft Connemara lilt wraps itself around my ears and my head, down into the earliest remembrances of me.

"He was weak, Mam. Few sounds dribbled out of him. I did not know he could not speak or swallow. I gave him a bit of millionaire's shortbread and he choked on it. I am so terribly sorry. I didn't mean to kill him. I wanted to come here to tell him I was sorry for being a terrible daughter, that it wasn't his fault I am the way I am. He did his best. He raised me the only way he knew how and he only wanted the best for me and I defied him. I'm so sorry Mam. Will he die?"

"Oh Mary, this has happened before. He choked last week on a biscuit he literally grabbed out of the hand of a visitor's child. He has been in and out of hospital. He pulls out the drips and the feeding tubes. He gets himself worked up into a state, but, then you remember what he was always like. He hated fuss. And he wanted everything done his way or not at all. I phone every week. I always ask if you have been to visit. But we haven't seen or heard from you in several years now.

"What has happened to my poor girl that I have not heard from you in so many years? I suppose you've been having far too much fun to be wasting your time thinking about your old Mother?"

Out of me comes all the sadness, the heart-breaking aloneness. I tell her I have a child; about the caravan, the croft, the man I thought would look after us; how I used him. I tell her you were stolen and I have only just rescued you. I hear her slump then click on her computer. At last, the bones of my disasters are laid bare.

"I am booking a flight," she says.

As I speak she surfs the internet. She clicks and taps and types.

"You must go back," she says, "The healing; the learning is in the circle. But I will help you. Stay there for a few days. Look after him. Tell him the things you need to. Make sure he doesn't die yet. Talk to the tree. Show your daughter the places I showed you. Then meet me at the airport in Inverness at lunchtime on Friday. I'll bring my own food! We will return to the island. You can tell me all about it then and I will show you how to use the strength I gave you."

Mothers, like rocks and standing stones, rarely change.

* * *

The chin is bristly. I am spiked by a hundred needles. My Father's face remains unshaven, my cheek reddens.

"I love you Daddy," I tell him.

You are sprawled at the bottom of the bed. Pencils, crayons and paper littered everywhere. We have already found a use for the surgical tape, and the space around him has been transformed into a gallery. You drew rainbows and mountains.

"I am so sorry, Daddy. I am sorry I gave you the biscuit. I am a terrible daughter. You taught me better and I should know better. Can you forgive me please?"

My arms are around his neck. I whisper and sob in his ear. Half of his face is frozen. He croaks and gurgles. People march up and down outside his room, they are carrying laundry and food to and from the other rooms. We hear the television blaring Deal or no Deal. We hear the cries of an old woman searching for her Mother. She calls and calls pleading for her Mother to come and help her. There is no relief for her. She is offered many cups of tea. A telephone rings loudly. A drug trolley rattles by. My Dad is given antacids and cardiac pills. He seems bitterly disappointed with the mediocre medicines. His face crumples. I think I see a sneer. I think he is suffering. I think he wants it to end.

I find a basin and fill it with warm water. I put a towel around his shoulders and make lather from soap, sweep the suds up onto the brush then circle his face with foam. I glide the razor along his neck. Up and down. Rinse and repeat. I make the skin taut under his nose just as he showed me when I was ten. He is the only man I have ever shaved.

I wipe him clean with warm, damp flannels. I rub oil in his skin. I clean the basin, bring fresh warm water. I put his hands into the basin. I bought a little nail brush and I scrub at his fingers. I uncurl his clenched fingers, massage oil along the length of his palm, stretch the withered digits; soothe the ache out of them.

"Is that better Daddy?"

He thumps me on the arm, points down at his feet, waggles one leg, sticks a filthy foot out from underneath the blanket. The toenails are long, yellow and pointy.

"A chiropodist would have to do your feet. I wouldn't be qualified. I can only do the wee jobs."

He knows it's an excuse, looks at me with watery grey eyes – 'you're not that sorry' they seem to say. He shrugs and points to his bedside cabinet instead.

"Book," he says, and there it is. The other book we had at home – The Bible. We had the entire collection of the works of Shakespeare and The Bible. Both were quoted ad nauseum. The rules I learnt were based on the hierarchy within the sexes. I hand him the Bible. He takes my left hand and points at my ring finger, makes the gurgling clicking noise again and begins to turn a bit red.

I cannot tell him I am unable to love men; that I am not made that way. I cannot tell him I love another woman. I don't want to upset him. I don't want to offend him and his religious beliefs. He places the Bible in my hand. Through mumbles and gestures I learn it is a present. A gift for you from your Granddad and I am to read it to you, teach you as he taught me. He reads my face, my unconvinced smile of acquiescence. I have read the book many times, searched for the laws that forbade homosexuality and never found them. I read the Word of God and never understood why I was deemed so sinful. He cast me out of his home many years ago: the day my Mother drove her car into Loch Tay, the day I told them I was gay. From then until now I have hidden myself away.

"I spoke to Mum," I say.

He exhales with a wheeze. A sigh of pain. He dips his head.

"She's in Spain," I continue. He nods.

"I am meeting her in Inverness on Friday. Angie and I have nowhere to live and she is going to help us find someplace. We will go back to the island. The house here is rented out."

It is rented out to pay the nursing home fees. If he died then you and Winnie and Woof and I could live there. If I told him about Winnie he may die. But I don't. I don't mention her. She lies in my heart as though she were asleep in my arms.

He points again to his bedside cabinet, makes motions for me to fetch some other thing. I go and pick up his various belongings. First a comb with missing teeth, then the plastic cup in which he keeps his dentures. In a drawer is a photo of Mum and me, but that is not what he wants.

Finally, when I show him his wallet he smiles with half his face; one eye rising slightly, the other flaccid and fallen. He cannot hold his wallet in the one good hand and coins spill out onto the bed. You reach and grab them and hand them over to him. He gives them back to you. With garbled vowels he bids me take his cash. There's a few hundred pounds and he wants me to have it. I don't say I need more, much more than a few hundred pounds. I debate whether or not to ask him for a few thousand, but I resist. I take his cash and I thank him. I tell him it will make a huge difference in our lives. There is then nothing left to say or do. I hug him. You hug him.

"Thank you Grandpa for the money." You say. You hand him your masterpiece; a picture of you and him sitting drawing pictures with Winnie and I on either side.

We see a tiny tear trapped in his eyelashes.

15

MOTHERS HEARTS

"Oh Mary, what have you done to your hair? When was the last time you had a haircut? And your clothes! Oh Dear God! Look at the poor child. Oh my poor wee little Angel, you are the image of your Mother, God help you."

My Mother, I had forgotten she doesn't pause for breath. She talks and talks and talks. She has only just emerged into the Arrivals Hall of Inverness Airport. This is her greeting. She berates me constantly.

"What are you both wearing? These clothes look like rags; like someone else's cast-offs. Mother of Christ, I taught you better than this. You are a fine looking woman; you come from good genes, why have you let yourself go?"

I haven't seen her in seven years. She is, of course, immaculate. She looks like she has just stepped out of a beauty salon. She does not look like she has spent twenty four hours travelling, taken three flights and been delayed time and time again.

"We will have to go shopping. I haven't been shopping in Inverness for many years. Come to me, wee one, I am your Granny, but call me Abuela, that's Spanish, I will teach you Spanish, a lovely language, I am the one in charge now."

She produces a mobile from her bag. She googles 'hairdressers in Inverness' and she walks off, we have to follow, we have to obey. I take her bags. You take her hand. You look up at her, silent and smiling. I can't help it. I smile too.

"This is a bus. Do you not have a car? And it isn't clean. Have you been living in this bus?"

She brushes bridie crumbs from the passenger seat. She finds an empty plastic bag and picks up all the rubbish, puts it in the bag.

"You'll need your eyebrows done."

I am grinning now. The dog cowers a little. She stays at the back of the bus, head down.

"Give me your phone. I want to contact this boy's Mother. I need to know exactly what has happened. It is time for the Mothers to take charge."

I hand her the phone Winnie gave me. My Mother reads our messages. She sighs and clicks and tuts. I drive into Inverness. My Mum phones Elsie first, scribbles down notes on the back of an envelope then phones Gertrude. Gertrude has been in Totnes for a few days. She is overcome with remorse. I can hear her cry. She apologises over and over again to my Mother, but declines to speak with me. My Mother nods and grunts, occasionally she says 'shocking behaviour' or 'appalling way to behave'. After a while the conversation turns to 'time to grow up.'

My Mother commiserates with Gertrude. She is polite, attentive; courteous. The she turns to me and says:

"Stop the bus. I want to look at my grandchild."

I pull over in a lay-by outside the city.

"She is beautiful, Mary."

My Mother peers round at you as you snore.

"She is the living image of you. You were, and still are, the greatest blessing ever bestowed on your Father and I. You know that you were a twin, don't you? I miscarried late on in pregnancy. You had a twin brother. Your Father and I wondered, for many years whether you had absorbed some of his male genes while growing inside me. You were such a tomboy. Mary, my own beautiful daughter, we knew you were a little different ever before you did. We knew you would never settle with a man, any man. We accepted that. We saw it simply as who you were. We had to let you go and find your own way. It was hard for us, but we wanted you to find your own happiness. You will have to do the same for your own daughter some day. You were born to be as you are, I understand you had to find out for yourself and please God, you have. Please God you know who you are now and what you must do.

"We taught you to be honest. We taught you to do the right thing. You are a brave, intelligent, loving woman. You have made mistakes and learned from them. You are just like all the other brave wonderful Mothers that raise their children day after day come what may."

She reaches out and strokes my hair, then looks for split ends.

"I taught you how to dress yourself. I taught you to look after your body. I told you how important this was. I want you to promise me that you will look after yourself when I am not here, in the manner in which I have taught you. You are a fine looking woman, honour that, honour the genetics that allow you that luxury. You are strong, independent and more than capable of doing whatever you set your mind to – respect that gift. You have enough love in your heart for the whole world, but do not waste it on those that wish to take it from you. Choose wisely whom to love.

"Sex itself is a great act, but love making is far more satisfying. You are well educated and articulate, do not hide yourself away thinking others are better. You are my daughter. I have raised you, I know you better than you know yourself. It is your responsibility to respect and honour me, as it will be Angie's duty to do as she has been taught. This family you were mixed up with have none of the advantages you had. They were destroyed early, by separation, by insecurity. Leave them alone, to heal. You must get on with your own life and I will always be just a phone call and a plane ride away."

My ears are open Mother, I can hear you. I remember where I came from, where I got all the love – my Mother the tiger.

My hair is cut into a bob. Your hair is cut into a bob. We are little and large images of each other. My eyebrows are waxed. I had a facial. My nails are clean and shapely. I declined the pedicure. I was afraid of the verbal onslaught that would surely ensue if I took off my boots. I will have to find a way to wash my feet in private, before we go back to the caravan. Oh No, the caravan! I cannot expect my Mother to stay in the caravan. And I cannot keep it as a shock. I will have to tell her. Maybe you should tell her.

You have been very quiet. You just hold Granny's hand and smile and do as you are told.

"Mum, I have been living in a caravan. It is rotten. You won't like it. Anyway, I will have to move out. I can't stay there."

"Yes," She says, "I have been thinking about that. You are entitled to a council house, Mary. I will stay until I see you set up nicely. The money I have saved can go towards making you and Angel comfortable. We will stay in the city tonight. Then I will find us a nice hotel on the island, with a good view of the sea and the mountains and we will go to the Council and have you re-homed. I will mind my wee little Angel while you go yourself to the caravan, I do not want to even see it, and you can get whatever stuff you need. Then we will talk about setting you up in some sort of decent employment and finding a nursery place for my wee Angel. Doesn't she look better now, see her pretty face?"

And she bends over and kisses you. And you; you take your still-podgy hands, place them on either side of her face and kiss her, full on the lips.

"We will have to look at carpets," she says, as though, in her mind, we are already re-homed.

"You will need a good bed each. You will need a television, a DVD and some cartoons. You will need a bookcase, a couch you can both sit in to read to each other. Mary, if we could get you a house with a spare room, you could take in clients for beauty treatments. You were good at that once upon a time. It would bring you in a bit of money. It would give you back a bit of self esteem. It would make you look after yourself. And it would be terribly handy, for when I come to stay.

"Have you got decent pots and pans? Have you got good crockery, the way you can offer clients a cup of tea? Oh, we will have to get these things. I can only imagine what sort of mugs you have, chipped no doubt, like a builder would drink out of. And towels – sure, you'll need new towels too. I have money. But first of all, daughter mine, we are getting you new shoes. Those boots are dreadful. Did you find them in a bin because that is exactly where they belong?"

My Mother, my daughter, my dog and I go shoe shopping. I have to reveal my feet. She takes the old steel toe cap work boots I found at Gertrude's back door and she asks the shop assistant for two black bags, so that she can double-bag them before unceremoniously dumping them in a litter bin.

"Don't be teaching my wee little Angel your terrible ways. Teach her how to care for herself. That way she can care for others. That way, others will care for her. Now, you'll need some good bras in Marks n Sparks. Come on, we'll have some lunch soon, when I can be sure of sitting down comfortably in a restaurant with you, without people giving me funny looks. Anyway, ye are looking better already. God, your hair was like a whin bush, it's so much smarter like that. And you look younger. I will put money in your account every month or so for hair cuts for the pair of ye. And, for God's sake text me when she needs shoes and I will send her some. Don't let her wear wellies her whole life."

She prattles on and on and on. I nod and smile in all the right places. You grin. You haven't let go of her hand. Woof sniffs her, licks her.

"…And we will get snowdrops and plant them in your garden. It's a bit late, but, sure never mind, they might come up. And every year, as winter ends, as the snow melts, and the days get a stretch in them, you will see the delicate white head of the first flower, bringing a reminder, year on year, that the cycle of life goes on. No matter what happens, no matter what the year throws at you, Spring always comes. Hold Love in your heart Mary, and it will come back to you, time and time again."

THE JANUARY FLOWER

You are at school as I write this. Your books, dolls and pens are scattered all around the living room floor. Woof snores under the table; at my feet. She would like a walk on the beach and rather than remembering this two year tale, I should be out, throwing sticks into the water for her. Rather than recalling my lesson, I should be tidying this house, our home. I could go out in the garden and pick some snowdrops, put them in a vase, take a picture and post it on Facebook for my Mother. But, instead, I am writing another chapter for the great novel of our lives.

The social worker helped us find this place. She helped me find my place. The lady from Working For Families had documented our conversation. She came to see me. Her name is Maggie. She helped me set up a little cleaning business, with the emphasis on ecologically friendly, homemade cleaning solutions! Maggie says that creativity can help relax our minds, so I started to write this book.

We were lucky. We got a house by the beach. There are trees at the back of the garden. I built a climbing frame, made a swing from an old tyre. Kids come, most days, to laugh and play and run with you. From here I can watch the waves, the oyster catchers and the otters. You can walk to school, hand in hand with me.

You can skip to the shore. You feed the local robin, another bossy little bird, which comes into the house if the door or window is left open.

A year has come and gone. I never heard from Winnie or Wallace. I have never seen Gertrude in the shop or in the town. I met another woman though, at a book club. I think it may be love, but only time will tell.

First, you can grow in Nature, as I did.

Lightning Source UK Ltd.
Milton Keynes UK
UKOW05f1344310117
293284UK00008B/230/P